DEATH AT INTERVALS

José Saramago was born in Portugal in 1922 and became a full-time writer in 1979. His oeuvre embraces plays, poetry, short stories, non-fiction and over a dozen novels, which have been translated into forty languages and have established him as one of Portugal's most influential writers. In 1998 he was awarded the Nobel Prize for Literature. José Saramago died on 18 June 2010.

Margaret Jull Costa has translated works by Eça de Queiroz, Fernando Pessoa, and José Régio, as well as a number of leading Spanish writers. Her translation of José Saramago's *All the Names* won the Weidenfeld Translation Prize.

ALSO BY JOSÉ SARAMAGO
IN ENGLISH TRANSLATION

Fiction

The Manual of Painting and Calligraphy
Baltasar and Blimunda
The Year of the Death of Ricardo Reis
The Gospel According to Jesus Christ
The History of the Siege of Lisbon
Blindness
All the Names
The Tale of the Unknown Island
The Stone Raft
The Cave
The Double
The Elephant's Journey

Non-Fiction

Journey to Portugal

JOSÉ SARAMAGO

Death at Intervals

TRANSLATED FROM THE PORTUGESE BY
Margaret Jull Costa

VINTAGE BOOKS
London

Published by Vintage 2008

8 10 9

Copyright © José Saramago and Editorial Caminho S.A., Lisbon 2005
English translation copyright © Margaret Jull Costa 2008

José Saramago has asserted his right under the Copyright, Designs
and Patents Act 1988 to be identified as the author of this work

First published in Great Britain in 2008 by Harvill Secker

Vintage
Random House, 20 Vauxhall Bridge Road,
London, SW1V 2SA

www.vintage-books.co.uk

Addresses for companies within The Random House Group Limited can be
found at: www.randomhouse.co.uk/offices.htm

The Random House Group Limited Reg. No. 954009

A CIP catalogue record for this book
is available from the British Library

ISBN 9780099502487

Funded by the Portuguese Institute for Books and Libraries

MINISTÉRIO DA CULTURA

INSTITUTO PORTUGUÊS DO
LIVRAO E DAS BIBLIOTECAS

MIX
Paper from
responsible sources
FSC
www.fsc.org   FSC® C016897

Printed and bound in Great Britain by Clays Ltd, St Ives PLC

Translator's acknowledgements

I would like to thank José Saramago, Tânia Ganho, Ben Sherriff and Maartje de Kort for all their help and advice.

For Pilar, my home

We will know less and less what it means to be human.

Book of Predictions

If, for example, you were to think more deeply about death, then it would be truly strange if, in so doing, you did not encounter new images, new linguistic fields.

Wittgenstein

THE FOLLOWING DAY, NO ONE DIED. THIS FACT, BEING ABSOLUTELY contrary to life's rules, provoked enormous and, in the circumstances, perfectly justifiable anxiety in people's minds, for we have only to consider that in the entire forty volumes of universal history there is no mention, not even one exemplary case, of such a phenomenon ever having occurred, for a whole day to go by, with its generous allowance of twenty-four hours, diurnal and nocturnal, matutinal and vespertine, without one death from an illness, a fatal fall, or a successful suicide, not one, not a single one. Not even from a car accident, so frequent on festive occasions, when blithe irresponsibility and an excess of alcohol jockey for position on the roads to decide who will reach death first. New year's eve had failed to leave behind it the usual calamitous trail of fatalities, as if old atropos with her great bared teeth had decided to put aside her shears for a day. There was, however, no shortage of blood. Bewildered, confused, distraught, struggling to control their feelings of nausea, the firemen extracted from the mangled remains wretched human bodies that, according to the mathematical logic of the collisions, should have been well and truly dead, but which, despite the seriousness of the injuries and lesions suffered, remained alive and were carried off to hospital, accompanied by the shrill sound of the ambulance sirens. None of these people would die along the way and all would disprove the most pessimistic of medical prognoses, There's nothing to be done for the poor man, it's not even worth operating, a

1

complete waste of time, said the surgeon to the nurse as she was adjusting his mask. And the day before, there would probably have been no salvation for this particular patient, but one thing was clear, today, the victim refused to die. And what was happening here was happening throughout the country. Up until the very dot of midnight on the last day of the year there were people who died in full compliance with the rules, both those relating to the nub of the matter, i.e. the termination of life, and those relating to the many ways in which the aforementioned nub, with varying degrees of pomp and solemnity, chooses to mark the fatal moment. One particularly interesting case, interesting because of the person involved, was that of the very ancient and venerable queen mother. At one minute to midnight on the thirty-first of december, no one would have been so ingenuous as to bet a spent match on the life of the royal lady. With all hope lost, with the doctors helpless in the face of the implacable medical evidence, the royal family, hierarchically arranged around the bed, waited with resignation for the matriarch's last breath, perhaps a few words, a final edifying comment regarding the moral education of the beloved princes, her grandsons, perhaps a beautiful, well-turned phrase addressed to the ever ungrateful memory of future subjects. And then, as if time had stopped, nothing happened. The queen mother neither improved nor deteriorated, she remained there in suspension, her frail body hovering on the very edge of life, threatening at any moment to tip over onto the other side, yet bound to this side by a tenuous thread to which, out of some strange caprice, death, because it could only have been death, continued to keep hold. We had passed over to the next day, and on that day, as we said at the beginning of this tale, no one would die.

It was already late afternoon when the rumour began to spread that, since the beginning of the new year, or more precisely since zero hours on this first day of january, there was no record in the whole country of anyone dying. You might think, for example, that the rumour had its origins in the queen mother's surprising resistance to giving up the little life that was left to her, but the truth is that the usual medical bulletin issued to the media by the palace's press office not only stated that the general state of the royal patient had shown visible signs of improvement during the night, it even suggested, indeed implied, choosing its words very carefully, that there was a chance that her royal highness might be restored to full health. In its initial form, the rumour might also have sprung, naturally enough, from an undertaker's, No one seems to want to die on this first day of the new year, or from a hospital, That fellow in bed twenty-seven can't seem to make up his mind one way or the other, or from a spokesman for the traffic police, It's really odd, you know, despite all the accidents on the road, there hasn't been a single death we can hold up as a warning to others. The rumour, whose original source was never discovered, although, of course, this hardly mattered in the light of what came afterwards, soon reached the newspapers, the radio and the television, and immediately caused the ears of directors, assistant directors and editors-in-chief to prick up, for these are people not only primed to sniff out from afar the major events of world history, they're also trained in the ability, when it suits, to make those events seem even more major than they really are. In a matter of minutes, dozens of investigative journalists were out on the street asking questions of any joe soap who happened by, while the ranks of telephones in the throbbing editorial offices stirred and trembled in an identical investigatory frenzy. Calls were made to hospitals, to the red cross, to the morgue, to funeral directors, to the police, yes, all of them, with the understandable exception of the secret branch, but the replies given could be

3

summed up in the same laconic words, There have been no deaths. A young female television reporter had more luck when she interviewed a passer-by, who kept glancing alternately at her and at the camera, and who described his personal experience, which was identical to what had happened to the queen mother, The church clock was striking midnight, he said, when, just before the last stroke, my grandfather, who seemed on the very point of expiring, suddenly opened his eyes as if he'd changed his mind about the step he was about to take, and didn't die. The reporter was so excited by what she'd heard that, ignoring all his pleas and protests, No, senhora, I can't, I have to go to the chemist's, my grandfather's waiting for his prescription, she bundled him into the news car, Come with me, your grandfather doesn't need prescriptions any more, she yelled, and ordered the driver to go straight to the television studio, where, at that precise moment, everything was being set up for a debate between three experts on paranormal phenomena, namely, two highly regarded wizards and a celebrated clairvoyant, hastily summoned to analyse and give their views on what certain wags, the kind who have no respect for anything, were already beginning to refer to as a death strike. The bold reporter was, however, labouring under the gravest of illusions, for she had interpreted the words of her interviewee as meaning that the dying man had, quite literally, changed his mind about the step he was about to take, namely, to die, cash in his chips, kick the bucket, and so had decided to turn back. Now, the words that the happy grandson had pronounced, As if he'd changed his mind, were radically different from a blunt, He changed his mind. An elementary knowledge of syntax and a greater familiarity with the elastic subtleties of tenses would have avoided this blunder, as well as the subsequent dressing-down that the poor girl, scarlet with shame and humiliation, received from her immediate superior.

Little could they, either he or she, have imagined that these words, repeated live by the interviewee and heard again in recorded form on that evening's news bulletin, would be interpreted in exactly the same mistaken way by millions of people, and that an immediate and disconcerting consequence of this would be the creation of a group firmly convinced that with the simple application of will power they, too, could conquer death and that the undeserved disappearance of so many people in the past could be put down solely to a deplorable weakness of will on the part of previous generations. But things would not stop there. People, without having to make any perceptible effort, continued not to die, and so another popular mass movement, endowed with a more ambitious vision of the future, would declare that humanity's greatest dream since the beginning of time, the happy enjoyment of eternal life here on earth, had become a gift within the grasp of everyone, like the sun that rises every day and the air that we breathe. Although the two movements were both competing, so to speak, for the same electorate, there was one point on which they were able to agree, and that was on the nomination as honorary president, given his eminent status as pioneer, of the courageous veteran who, at the final moment, had defied and defeated death. As far as anyone knows, no particular importance would be given to the fact that grandpa remains in a state of profound coma, which everything seems to indicate is irreversible.

Although the word crisis is clearly not the most appropriate one to describe these extraordinary events, for it would be absurd, incongruous and an affront to the most basic logic to speak of a crisis in an existential situation that has been privileged by the absence of death, one can understand why some citizens, zealous of their right to know the truth, are asking themselves, and each other, what the hell is going on with the government, who have so far given not the slightest sign of life. When asked in passing during a brief interval between two meetings, the minister for health, had, it is true, explained to journalists that, bearing in mind that they lacked sufficient information to form a judgement, any official statement would, inevitably, be premature, We are collating data being sent to us from all over the country, he added, and it's true to say that no deaths have been reported, but, as you can imagine, we have been as surprised as everyone else by this turn of events and are not as yet ready to formulate an initial theory about the origins of the phenomenon or about its immediate and future implications. He could have left the matter there, which, considering the difficulties of the situation, would have been a cause for gratitude, but the well-known impulse to urge people to keep calm about everything and nothing and to remain quietly in the fold whatever happens, this tropism which, amongst politicians, especially if they're in government, has become second nature, not to say automatic or mechanical, led him to conclude the conversation in the worst possible way, As minister responsible for health, I can assure everyone listening that there is absolutely no reason for alarm, If I understand you correctly, remarked the journalist in a tone that tried hard not to appear too ironic, the fact that no one is dying is, in your view, not in the least alarming, Exactly, well, those may not have been my precise words, but, yes, that, essentially, is what I said, May I remind you, minister, that people were dying even yesterday and it would never have occurred to anyone to think that alarming, Of course not, it's normal to die, and dying only becomes alarming when deaths multiply, during a war or an epidemic, for example, When things depart from the norm, You could put it like that, yes, But in the current situation, when, apparently, no one is prepared to die, you call on us not to be alarmed, would you not agree with me,

6

minister, that such an appeal is, at the very least, somewhat paradoxical, It was mere force of habit, and I recognise that I shouldn't have applied the word alarm to the current situation, So what word would you use, minister, I only ask because, as the conscientious journalist I hope I am, I always try, where possible, to use the exact term. Slightly irritated by the journalist's insistence, the minister replied abruptly, I would use not one word, but six, And what would those be, minister, Let us not foster false hopes. This would doubtless have provided a good, honest headline for the newspaper the following day, but the editor-in-chief, having consulted his managing editor, thought it inadvisable, from the business point of view as well, to throw this bucket of icy water over the prevailing mood of enthusiasm, Let's go for the usual headline, New Year, New Life, he said.

In the official communiqué, broadcast late that night, the prime minister confirmed that no deaths had been recorded anywhere in the country since the beginning of the new year, he called for moderation and a sense of responsibility in any evaluations and interpretations of this strange fact, he reminded people that one could not exclude the hypothesis that this was merely a fluke, a freak cosmic change that could not possibly last, an exceptional conjunction of coincidences impinging on the space-time equation, but that, just in case, the government had already begun exploratory talks with the relevant international organisations to enable the government, when necessary, to take efficient, coordinated action. Having uttered this pseudoscientific flim-flam, whose very incomprehensibility was intended to calm the commotion gripping the nation, the prime minister ended by stating that the government was prepared for all humanly imaginable eventualities, and determined to face with courage and with the vital support of the population the complex social, economic, political and moral problems that the definitive extinction of death would inevitably provoke, if, as everything seemed to indicate, this situation was confirmed. We will accept the challenge of the body's immortality, he exclaimed in exalted tones, if that is the will of god, to whom we will always offer our grateful prayers for having chosen the good people of this country as his instrument. Which means, thought the prime minister when he finished reading the statement, that the noose is well and truly round our necks. Little did he imagine how tightly that noose would be drawn. Not half an hour had passed when, sitting now in the official car taking him home, he received a call from the cardinal, Good evening, prime minister, Good evening, your eminence, Prime minister, I'm phoning to tell you that I feel profoundly shocked, Oh, so do I, your eminence, it's an extremely grave situation, the gravest situation the country has ever had to confront, That's not what I mean, What do you mean, your eminence, It is utterly deplorable that when you wrote the statement I have just listened to, you failed to remember what constitutes the foundation, the main beam, the cornerstone, the keystone of our holy religion, Forgive me, your eminence, but I can't quite see what you're driving at, Without death, prime minister, without death there is no resurrection, and without resurrection there is no church, Hell's bells, Sorry, I didn't quite hear what you said, could you say that again, please, Me, no, I said nothing, your eminence, it was probably some interference on the line caused by atmospheric electricity, by static, or even a problem with reception, the satellite does sometimes cut out, but you were saying, your eminence, Yes, I was saying that any catholic, and you are no exception, must know that without resurrection there is no church, more than that, how could it even occur to you that god would ever will his own demise, such an idea is pure sacrilege, possibly the very worst of blasphemies, Your eminence, I didn't say that god had willed his own demise, Not in those exact words, no, but you admitted the possibility that the immortality of the body might be the will of god, and one doesn't need a doctorate in transcendental logic to realise that it comes down to the same thing, Your eminence, believe me, I only said it for effect, to make an impression, it was just a way of rounding off the speech, that's all, you know how important these things are in politics, Such things are just as important in the church, prime minister, but we think hard before we open our mouths, we don't just talk for talking's sake, we calculate the long-term effects, indeed, our speciality, if you'd like me to give you a useful image, is ballistics, Well, I'm very sorry, your eminence, If I was in your shoes, I'd be sorry too. As if estimating how long the grenade would take to fall, the cardinal paused, then, in a gentler, friendlier tone, went on, May I ask if you showed the statement to his majesty before reading it out for the media, Naturally, your eminence, dealing, as the statement did, with such a very ticklish subject, And what did the king say, assuming, of course, that it's not a state secret, He thought it was fine, Did he make any comment after he'd read it, Excellent, What do you mean excellent, That's what his majesty said, excellent, Do you mean that he, too, blasphemed, Your eminence, it is not up to me to make such judgements, living with my own mistakes is quite hard enough, Well, I will have to speak to the king and remind him that in a confusing and delicate situation like this, only faithful, unswerving observance of the proven doctrine of our holy mother church can save the country from the dreadful chaos about to overwhelm us, That is up to you, your eminence, that is your role, Yes, I will ask his majesty which he prefers, to see the queen mother for ever dying, prostrate on a bed from which she will never again rise, with her earthly body shame-fully clinging to her soul, or to see her, by dying, triumph over death, in the eternal, splendid glory of the heavens, Surely no one would hesitate over which answer to give, Probably not, but, contrary to what you may think, prime minister, I care less about the answers than I do about the questions, notice that our questions have both an obvious objective and a hidden intention, and when we ask them, it is not only so that the person being questioned gives the answers which, at that moment, we need him to hear himself saying, it is also in order to prepare the way for future answers, A bit like politics, your eminence, Exactly, except that unlikely though it may seem, the advantage the church has is that by managing what is on high, it governs what is down below. There was another pause, which was interrupted by the prime minister, I'm nearly home, your eminence, but if I may, there is one question I would like to ask you, Ask away, What will the church do if no one ever dies again, Never is too long a time, even when one is dealing with death, prime minister, You have not, I feel, answered my question, your eminence, Let me turn the question back on you, what will the state do if no one ever dies again, The state will try to survive, although I very much doubt it will, but the church, The church, prime minister, has grown so accustomed to eternal answers that I can't imagine it giving any other kind, Even if reality contradicts them, We've done nothing but contradict reality from the outset, and yet we're still here, What will the pope say, If I were pope, and god forgive me the ridiculous vanity of imagining such a thing, I would immediately issue a new thesis, that of death postponed, With no further explanations, The church has never been asked to explain anything, our speciality, along with ballistics, has always been the neutralisation of the overly curious mind through faith, Goodnight, your eminence, see you tomorrow, God willing, prime minister, god willing, Given the way things are at the moment, it doesn't look like he has much choice, Don't forget, prime minister, that beyond the frontiers of our country, people continue to die as normal, which is a good sign, That depends on your point of view, your eminence, perhaps they're viewing us as a kind of oasis, a garden, a new paradise, Or a new hell, if they've got any sense, Goodnight, your eminence, I wish you a peaceful, restoring night's sleep, Goodnight, prime minister, and if death does decide to return tonight, I hope she doesn't think to visit you, If justice is anything more than an empty word, the queen mother should go before I do, Well, I promise I won't denounce you to the king tomorrow, That's very good of you, your eminence, Goodnight, Goodnight.

It was three o'clock in the morning when the cardinal had to be rushed into hospital with an attack of acute appendicitis which required immediate surgery. Before he was sucked down the tunnel of anaesthesia, in the fleeting moment that precedes a total loss of consciousness, he thought what so many others have thought, that he might die during the operation, then he remembered that this was no longer a possibility, and in one final flash of lucidity, he thought, too, that if, despite everything, he did die, that would mean, paradoxically, that he had vanquished death. Filled by an irresistible desire for sacrifice, he was about to beg god to kill him, but did not have time to formulate the words. Anaesthesia saved him from the supreme sacrilege of wanting to transfer the powers of death to a god more generally known as a giver of life.

ALTHOUGH IT HAD IMMEDIATELY BEEN RIDICULED BY RIVAL newspapers, which had managed to draw on the inspiration of their principal writers for the most diverse and meaty of head-lines, some dramatic, some lyrical and others almost philo-sophical or mystical, if not touchingly ingenuous, as was the case with the popular newspaper that contented itself with And What Will Become Of Us Now, ending the phrase with the graphical flourish of an enormous question mark, the afore-mentioned headline New Year, New Life, for all its grating banality, had struck a real chord with some people who, for reasons either of nature or nurture, preferred the solidity of a more or less pragmatic optimism, even if they had reasons to suspect that it might be merely a vain illusion. Having lived, until those days of confusion, in what they had imagined to be the best of all possible and probable worlds, they were discov-ering, with delight, that the best, the absolute best, was happening right now, right there, at the door of their house, a unique and marvellous life without the daily fear of parca's creaking scissors, immortality in the land that gave us our being, safe from any metaphysical awkwardnesses and free to everyone, with no sealed orders to open at the hour of our death, announcing at that crossroads where dear companions in this vale of tears known as earth were forced to part and set off for their different destinations in the next world, you to paradise, you to purgatory, you down to hell. Because of this, the more reticent or more thoughtful newspapers, along with like-minded radio and television stations, had no option but to join the high tide of collective joy that was sweeping the country from north to south and from east to west, refreshing fearful minds and driving far from view the long shadow of thanatos. With the passing days, and when they saw that still no one died, pessimists and sceptics, only a few at a time at first, then en masse, threw in their lot with the mare magnum of citizens who took every opportunity to go out into the street and proclaim loudly that now life truly is beautiful.

One day, a lady, recently widowed, finding no other way of showing the new joy flooding her being, although not without a slight pang of grief to think that, if she did not die, she would never again see her much-mourned husband, had the idea of hanging the national flag from the flower-bedecked balcony of her dining-room. It was, as they say, no sooner said than done. In less than forty-eight hours the hanging out of flags had spread throughout the country, the colours and symbols of the flag took over the landscape, although more obviously so in the cities, of course, there being more balconies and windows in the city than in the country. Such patriotic fervour was impossible to resist, especially when certain worrying, not to say threatening statements, where they came from no one knew, began to be distributed, saying such things as, Anyone who doesn't hang our nation's immortal flag from the window of their house doesn't deserve to live, Anyone not displaying the national flag has sold out to death, Join us, be a patriot, buy a flag, Buy another one, Buy another, Down with the enemies of life, it's lucky for them that there's no more death. The streets were a veritable festival of fluttering insignia, flapping in the wind if it was blowing, and if wasn't, then a carefully positioned electric fan did the job, and if the fan wasn't powerful enough to make the standard flap in virile fashion, making those whipcrack noises that so exalt the martially minded, it would at least ensure that the patriotic colours undulated honourably. A small number of people murmured privately that it was completely over-the-top, a nonsense, and that sooner or later there would be no alternative but to remove all those flags and pennants, and the sooner the better, because just as too much sugar spoils the palate and harms the digestive process, so our normal and proper respect for patriotic emblems will become a mockery if we allow it to be perverted into this serial affront to modesty, on a par with those unlamented flashers in raincoats. Besides, they said, if the flags are there to celebrate the fact that death no longer kills, then we should do one of two things, either take them down before we get so fed up with them that we start to loathe our own national symbols, or else spend the rest of our lives, that is, eternity, yes, eternity, having to change them every time they start to rot in the rain or get torn to shreds by the wind or faded by the sun. There were very few people who had the courage to put their finger on the problem publicly, and one poor man had to pay for his unpatriotic outburst with a beating which, had death not ceased her operations in this country at the beginning of the year, would have put an end to his miserable life right there and then.

Nothing is ever perfect, however, for alongside those who laugh, there will always be others who weep, and sometimes, as in the present case, for the self-same reasons. Various important professions, seriously concerned about the situation, had already started to inform those in power of their discontent. As one would expect, the first formal complaints came from the undertaking business. Rudely deprived of their raw material, the owners began by making the classic gesture of putting their hands to their heads and wailing in mournful chorus, Now what's going to become of us, but then, faced by the prospect of a catastrophic collapse from which no one in the funeral trade would escape, they called a general meeting, at the end of which, after heated discussions, all of them unproductive because all of them, without exception, ran up against the indestructible wall of death's refusal to collaborate, the same death to which they had become accustomed, from parents down to children, as something which was their natural due, they finally approved a document to be submitted to the government for their consideration, which document adopted the only constructive proposal, well, constructive, but also hilarious, that had been presented at the debate, They'll laugh at us, warned the chairman, but I recognise that we have no other way out, it's either this or the ruin of the undertaking business. The document stated that, at an extraordinary general meeting called to examine the grave crisis they were going through because of the lack of deaths in the country, the funeral directors' representatives, after an intense and open debate, during which a respect for the supreme interests of the nation had always been paramount, had reached the conclusion that it was still possible to avoid the disastrous consequences of what would doubtless go down in history as the worst collective calamity to befall us since the founding of the nation, namely, that the government should make obligatory the burial or cremation of all domestic animals that die a natural or accidental death, and that such burials or cremations, regulated and approved, should be carried out by the funerary industry, bearing in mind our admirable work in the past as the public service which, in the deepest sense of the term, we have always been, generation after generation. The document went on, We would draw the government's attention to the fact that this vital change in the industry cannot be made without considerable financial investment, for it is not the same thing to bury a human being and to carry to its final resting-place a cat or a canary, or indeed a circus elephant or a bathtub crocodile, for it will require a complete reformulation of our traditional techniques, and the experience already acquired since pet cemeteries were given the official go-ahead will prove extremely useful in this essential process of modernisation, in other words, what has, up until now, been very much a side-line in our industry, although admittedly a very lucrative one, will now become our sole activity, thus avoiding, as far as possible, the dismissal of hundreds, if not thousands of self-less and courageous workers who have, every day of their working lives, bravely confronted the terrible face of death and upon whom death has now so unfairly turned her back, And so, prime minister, with a view to providing the protection merited by a profession which has, for millennia, been classi-fied as a public utility, we ask you to consider not only the urgent need for a favourable decision, but also, in parallel, either the opening of a line of subsidised loans or else, and this would be the icing on the cake, or perhaps I should say the brass handles on the coffin, not to say elementary justice, the granting of non-recoverable loans that would help towards the rapid revitalisation of a sector whose survival is now threatened for the first time in history, and, indeed, long before history began, in all the ages of pre-history as well, for no human corpse has ever lacked for someone who would, sooner or later, come along and bury it, even if it was only the generous earth herself opening up to receive it. Respectfully hoping that our request may be granted, we remain.

The directors and administrators of hospitals, both state-run and private, were soon beating on the door of the minister in question, the minister for health, to express, along with the other relevant public services, their worries and anxieties, which, strange though it may seem, always highlighted logis-tical rather than health matters. They stated that the usual rota-tional process of patients coming in, getting better or dying had suffered, if we may put it like this, a short-circuit or, if you prefer a less technical term, a bottleneck, the reason being the indefinite stay of an ever larger number of patients who, given the seriousness of their illnesses or of the accidents of which they had been victims, would, in the normal course of events, have passed over into the next life. The situation is extremely grave, they argued, we have already started putting patients out in the corridors, even more frequently than we usually do, and everything indicates that in less than a week's time, it will not only be the lack of beds we have to deal with, for with every corridor and every ward full, and given the lack of space and the difficulties of manoeuvring, we will have to face the fact that we have no idea where to put any beds that are available. There is a way of solving the problem, concluded the people in charge of the hospitals, however it does, very slightly, infringe the hippocratic oath, and the decision, were it to be taken, would have to be neither medical nor administrative, but political. Since a word to the wise is always enough, the minister for health, having consulted the prime minister, sent the following despatch, With regard to the unavoidable overcrowding which is already beginning to have a seriously prejudicial effect on the hitherto excellent working of our hospital system and which is a direct consequence of the growing number of people being admitted in a state of suspended life and who will remain so indefinitely with no possibility of a cure or even of any improvement, at least not until medical research reaches the new goals it has set itself, the government advises and recommends hospital boards and administrations that, following a rigorous analysis, on a case-by-case basis, of the clinical situation of patients who find themselves in this position, and once the irreversibility of those morbid processes has been confirmed, the patients should be handed over to the care of their families, with hospitals taking full responsibility for ensuring that patients receive all the treatments and examinations their GPs deem to be either necessary or advisable. The government's decision is based on a hypothesis within the grasp of everyone, namely that a patient in such a state, that is, permanently on the brink of a death which is permanently being denied to him, must, even during any brief moments of lucidity, be pretty much indifferent to where he is, whether in the loving bosom of his family or in a crowded hospital ward, given that, in neither place, will he manage to die or be restored to health. The government would like to take this opportunity to inform the population that investigations are continuing apace and these will, as we hope and trust, lead to a satisfactory understanding of the still mysterious causes of the disappearance of death. We would also like to say that a large interdisciplinary commission, including representatives from the various religions and philosophers from a variety of different schools of thought, who always have something to say about such matters, has been charged with the delicate task of reflecting on what a future without death will be like, at the same time trying to make a reasonable forecast of the new problems society will have to face, the principle of which some might summarise with this cruel question, What are we going to do with all the old people if death is not there to cut short any ambitions they may have to live an excessively long life.

Homes for the third and fourth age, those charitable institutions created for the peace of mind of families who have neither the time nor the patience to wipe away snot, tend to weary sphincters and get up at night to bring the bedpan, were not long in coming and beating their heads against the wailing wall, as the hospitals and undertakers had done before them. To give justice where justice is due, we should recognise that the dilemma in which they found themselves, namely, whether or not to continue taking in residents, would challenge the forward-planning skills of any manager of human resources, as well as any desire to be evenhanded. Largely because the final results, and this is what characterises genuine dilemmas, would always be the same. Accustomed until now, as were their querulous colleagues of the intravenous injection and the floral wreath with the purple ribbon, to the certainty resulting from the continuous and unstoppable rotation of lives and deaths, some coming in and others going out, the homes for the third and fourth ages did not even want to consider a working future in which the objects of their care never changed face or body, except to display them in a still more lamentable state with each day that passed, more decadent and more sadly dishevelled, the face growing steadily more shrivelled, line by line, like a raisin, limbs tremulous and hesitant, like a ship searching vainly for a compass that fell overboard. A new guest had always been a motive for celebration at these eventide homes, it meant a new name that one would have to fix in one's memory, particular habits brought from the outside world, eccentricities peculiar to them alone, like the retired civil servant who had to scrub his toothbrush every day because he couldn't bear seeing bits of toothpaste stuck among the bristles, or the old lady who drew family trees but could never find the right names to hang on the branches. For a few weeks, until routine evened out the amount of attention given to all the inmates, he or she would be the newcomer, the youngster, for the last time in his or her life, even if that life lasted as long as the eternity which, as people say of the sun, had come to shine on all the people of this fortunate land, on all of us who will see the sun set every day and yet remain alive, though no one knows how or why. Now, however, the new guest, unless he or she came to fill some vacancy and round up the institution's income, is someone whose fate is known beforehand, we won't see him leave here to go and die at home or in hospital as used to happen in the good old days, while the other residents hurriedly locked the door to their rooms so that death wouldn't enter and carry them off too, no, that, we know, is a thing of a past, a past that will never come back, but someone in government will have to consider our fate, us, the owners, managers and employees of these eventide homes, the fate awaiting us is that when the moment comes to down tools, there will be no one to take us in, we are not even masters of the thing which was, in a way, also ours, at least as regards the years of work we put in, and here, it should be pointed out, it was the employees' turn to speak, what we mean is that there will be no room for people like us in the eventide homes, unless we can rid ourselves of some of the residents, an idea that had already occurred to the government following the debate about the plethora of patients in hospitals, the family, they said, should resume its obligations, but for that to happen there would have to be at least one member of the family with sufficient intelligence and enough physical energy, gifts whose sell-by dates, as we know from our own experience and from what the world shows us, last only as long as a sigh when compared with this recently inaugurated eternity, anyway, the remedy, unless someone can come up with a better idea, would be to create more eventide homes, not as has been the case until now, using houses and mansions that have known better days, but building from scratch vast new edifices, in the form of a pentagon, for example, or a tower of babel or a labyrinth of knossos, starting out with districts, then cities, then metropoli, or, to put it more crudely, cemeteries of the living where fatal and irrenunciable old age will be cared for as god would have wanted until, since their days will have no end, who knows when, for the crux of the matter, and we feel it our duty to call this to the attention of the relevant authority, is that, with the passing of time, not only will there be more elderly people living in these eventide homes, but more and more people will be needed to care for them, with the result that the rhomboid of the ages will be swiftly turned on its head, with a gigantic, ever-growing mass of old people at the top, swallowing up like a python the new generations, who, transformed for the most part into nursing or administrative staff to work at these eventide homes, after spending the better part of their lives caring for old crocks of all ages, both the normally old and the methuselahs, multitudes of parents, grandparents, great-grandparents, great-great-grandparents, great-great-great-grandparents, and so on, ad infinitum, will, in turn, pile up, one on top of the other, like the leaves that fall from the trees onto the leaves from previous autumns, mais où sont les neiges d'antan, the endless throngs of those who, little by little, spent their lives losing teeth and hair, the legions with bad sight and bad hearing, those with hernias, colds, those with hip fractures, the paraplegic, the now immortal geriatrics who can't even stop the drool running down their chin, you, gentlemen of the government, may not want to believe us, but such a future is perhaps the worst nightmare that could ever have assailed a human being, such a thing would never have been seen even in the dark caves, where all was fear and trembling, and it is we who have had experience of the first eventide home who are saying this, and in those days, obviously, everything was very small-scale indeed, but our imaginations must serve for something, and to be perfectly frank, prime minister, hand on heart, rather death than such a destiny.

A terrible threat is endangering the survival of our industry, declared the president of the federation of insurance companies to the media, referring to the many thousands of letters which, all couched in more or less identical terms, as if they had been copied from a single draft, had, in the last few days, been flooding their offices, all calling for the immediate cancellation of the life insurance policies of the undersigned. These letters stated that, given the well-known fact that death had put an end to itself, it would be absurd, not to say down-right stupid, to continue paying exorbitant premiums which would only serve to make the companies still richer, with no kind of balancing recompense for them. I'm not pouring money down the drain, said one particularly disgruntled policy-holder in a postscript. Some went further, demanding the return of sums already paid, but in these cases, it was clear that they were just making a stab in the dark, trying their luck. In answer to the inevitable question from journalists about how the insurance companies intended to fend off this sudden salvo of heavy artillery, the president of the federation said that, while their legal advisors were, at that very moment, care-fully studying the small print of policies for some kind of inter-pretative loophole that would allow them, always keeping strictly to the letter of the law, of course, to impose on these heretical policy-holders, even if it were against their wishes, the obligation to continue paying premiums for as long as they remained alive, that is, for all eternity, the more likely option would be to reach some form of consensus, a gentlemen's agreement, which would consist in the addition to policies of a brief addendum, with one eye on rectifying the current situ-ation and with the other on the future, and which would set eighty as the age of obligatory death, in a purely figurative sense of course, the president was quick to add, smiling benev-olently. In this way, the companies would receive the premiums, as normal, until the date when the happy policy-holder cele-brated his eightieth birthday, at which time, now that he had become someone who was, virtually speaking, dead, he would promptly be paid the full sum stipulated in the policy. He should also add, and this would be of no small interest, that, if they so desired, customers could renew their contract for another eighty years, at the end of which, they would, to all intents and purposes, register a second death, and the earlier procedure would then be repeated, and so on and so forth. Amongst the journalists who knew their actuarial calculus, there were some admiring murmurs and a brief flutter of applause which the president acknowledged with a brief nod. Strategically and tactically, the move had been perfect, so much so that the following day letters started pouring in again to the insurance companies declaring the previous letters null and void. All the policy-holders declared themselves ready to accept the proposed gentleman's agreement, and indeed one might say, without exaggeration, that this was one of those very rare occasions when no one lost and everyone gained. Especially the insurance companies, which had been saved from catastrophe by the skin of their teeth. It is assumed that at the next election, the president of the federation will be re-elected to the post he fills so very brilliantly.

ONE CAN SAY ALMOST ANYTHING ABOUT THE FIRST MEETING OF the interdisciplinary commission except that it went well. The blame, if such a weighty term can be applied here, rests on the dramatic memorandum sent to the government by the eventide homes, especially those final ominous words, Rather death, prime minister, than such a destiny. The philosophers, divided as always between frowning pessimists and smiling optimists, readied themselves to recommence for the thousandth time the ancient dispute over whether the glass was half full or half empty, a dispute which, when transferred to the matter they had been summoned there to discuss, would probably come down to a mere inventory of the advantages and disadvantages of being dead or of living for ever, while the religious delegates, from the outset, presented a united front, hoping to set the debate on the only dialectical terrain that interested them, that is, the explicit acceptance that death was fundamental to the existence of the kingdom of god and that, therefore, any discussion about a future without death would be not only blasphemous but absurd, since it would, inevitably, presuppose an absent or, rather, vanished god. This was not a new attitude, the cardinal himself had already put his finger on the implications of this theological version of squaring the circle, when, in his phone conversation with the prime minister, he admitted, although not in so many words, that if there was no death, there could be no resurrection, and if there was no resurrection, then there would be no point in having a church. Now, since this was clearly the only agricultural implement god possessed with which to plough the roads that would lead to his kingdom, the obvious, irrefutable conclusion is that the entire holy story ends, inevitably, in a cul-de-sac. This bitter argument came from the mouth of the oldest of the pessimistic philosophers, who did not stop there, but went on, Whether we like it or not, the one justification for the existence of all religions is death, they need death as much as we need bread to eat. The religious delegates did not bother to protest. On the contrary, one of them, a highly regarded member of the catholic sector, said, You're absolutely right, my dear philosopher, that, of course, is why we exist, so that people will spend their entire life with fear hanging round their neck, and when their time comes, they will then welcome death as a liberation, You mean paradise, Paradise or hell, or nothing at all, what happens after death matters to us far less than is generally believed, religion, sir, is an earthly matter, and has nothing to do with heaven, That isn't what we're usually told, We had to say something to make the merchandise attractive, So does that mean you don't believe in eternal life, We pretend we do. For a minute no one spoke. The oldest of the pessimists allowed a wry smile to spread across his face and he adopted the air of someone who has just seen a particularly difficult laboratory experiment crowned with success. In that case, said a philosopher from the optimistic wing, why are you so alarmed by the fact that death has ended, We don't know that it has, we know only that it has ceased to kill, which is not the same thing, Agreed, but given that this doubt remains unresolved, I repeat my question, Because if human beings do not die then everything will be permissible, And would that be a bad thing, asked the old philosopher, As bad as nothing being permissible. There was another silence. The eight men seated round the table had been asked to reflect upon the consequences of a future without death and to construct from the present information a plausible forecast of what new problems a society would have to confront, quite apart, of course, from an inevitable exacerbation of the old problems. The trouble is that the future is already here, said one of the pessimists, before us we have, amongst others, statements drawn up by the so-called eventide homes, by hospitals, by funeral directors, by insurance companies, and apart from the latter, who will always find a way of profiting from any situation, one must admit that the prospects are not just gloomy, they're terrible, catastrophic, more dangerous by far than anything even the wildest imagination could dream up, Without wishing to be ironic, which, in the current circumstances, would be in appalling taste, remarked an equally highly regarded member of the protestant sector, it seems to me that this commission is dead before it's been born, The eventide homes are right, rather death than such a destiny, said the catholic spokesman, What do you propose we do then, asked the oldest of the pessimists, apart from the immediate dissolution of this commission, which is what you appear to want, We, the catholic apostolic roman church, will organise a national campaign of prayer, asking god to bring about the return of death as quickly as possible so as to save poor humanity from the worst horrors, Does god have authority over death, asked one of the optimists, They're two sides of the same coin, on one side the king and on the other the crown, In that case perhaps it was god who ordered death to withdraw, One day we will know why he set us this test, meanwhile we will put our rosaries to work, We will do the same, by which I mean that we, too, will pray, no rosaries for us, of course, smiled the protestant, And we will arrange processions throughout the country calling on death to return, just as we used to do ad petendam pluviam, to ask for rain, translated the catholic, We won't go that far,

26

such processions have never been part of our customs, said the protestant, smiling again, And what about us, asked one of the optimistic philosophers in a tone that seemed to announce his imminent enlistment in the ranks of the opposition, what are we going to do now, when it seems that all doors are closed to us, To start with, replied the oldest philosopher, let's adjourn this session, And then what, We will continue to philosophise since that is what we were born to do, even if all we have to philosophise about is the void, What for, I don't know what for, All right, then, why, Because philosophy needs death as much as religions do, if we philosophise it's in order to know that we will die, as monsieur de montaigne said, to philosophise is to learn how to die.

Even among those who were not philosophers, at least not in the usual meaning of the term, some had managed to learn that path. Paradoxically, they had not themselves learned how to die, because their time had not yet come, but to ease the deaths of others, by helping death. The method used, as you will soon see, was yet another manifestation of the human race's inexhaustible capacity for inventiveness. In a village, a few miles from the frontier with one of the neighbouring countries, there was a family of poor country people who, for their sins, had not one relative, but two, in that state of suspended life or, as they preferred to call it, arrested death. One of them was a grandfather of the old sort, a sturdy patriarch reduced by illness to a mere shadow, although it had not entirely robbed him of the power of speech. The other was a child of only a few months to whom they had not even had time to teach the words for life or death and to whom actual death had refused to show herself. They were neither dead nor alive, and the country doctor who visited them once a week said that there was nothing that could be done for or against them, not even by injecting each of them with a kindly lethal drug, which, not long ago, would have been the radical solution to such problems. At most, it might push them towards the place where death presumably was, but it would be pointless, futile, because at that precise moment, as unreachable as ever, she would take a step back and keep her distance. The family went to ask for help from the priest, who listened, raised his eyes to heaven and said that we are all in god's hands and that his divine mercy is infinite. Well, it might be infinite, but not infinite enough to help the poor little child who has done no wrong in this world. And that was how things stood, with no way forward, with no solution to the problem and no hope of finding one, when the old man spoke, Come over here someone, he said, Do you want a drink of water, asked one of his daughters, No, I don't want any water, I want to die, The doctor says that's not possible, papa, remember, no one dies anymore, The doctor doesn't know what he's talking about, ever since the world was world, there has always been an hour and a place to die, Not anymore, That's not true, Calm down, papa, you'll make your fever worse, I haven't got a fever and even if I had, it wouldn't matter, now listen to me carefully, All right, I'm listening, Come closer, before my voice gives out, What is it. The old man whispered a few words into his daughter's ear. She shook her head, but he insisted and insisted. But that won't solve anything, papa, she stammered, astonished and pale with horror, It will, And if it doesn't, We lose nothing by trying, And if it doesn't work, That's simple enough, you just bring me back home, And the child, The child goes too, and if I stay there, he stays with me. The daughter tried to think, her warring emotions etched on her face, then she asked, Why can't we bring you back and bury you both here, You can imagine how that would look, two deaths in a country where no one, however hard they try, can die, how would you explain that, besides, given the way things stand now, I'm not

28

sure death would allow us to return, It's madness, papa, Maybe, but I don't see any other way out of this situation, We want you alive, not dead, Yes, but not in my current state, alive but dead, dead but apparently alive, If that's what you want, we'll do as you ask, Give me a kiss. The daughter kissed him on the forehead and left the room, crying. With her face still bathed in tears, she went and told the rest of the family about her father's plan, that they should take him, that same night, across the border, where death was still functioning and where, or so he believed, death would have no alternative but to accept him. This announcement was received with a complicated mixture of pride and resignation, pride because it is not every day that one sees an old man, of his own volition, offering himself up to elusive death, and resignation because they had nothing to lose either way, what could they do, you can't fight fate. It is said that one cannot have everything in life, and the courageous old man will leave behind him only a poor, honest family who will certainly always honour his memory. The family wasn't just this daughter who had left the room in tears and the child who had done no wrong in this world, there was another daughter too and her husband, the parents of three children who were all, fortunately, in good health, plus a maiden aunt who was long past marrying age. The other son-in-law, the husband of the daughter who left the room in tears, is living in a distant land, where he emigrated to earn a living, and tomorrow, he will discover that he has lost the only child he had and the father-in-law he loved. That's how life is, what it gives with one hand one day, it takes away with the other. We are more aware than anyone how unimportant it must seem this acount of the relationships in a family of country folk whom we will probably never see again, but it seemed to us wrong, even from a purely technical, narratorial point of view, to dismiss in two lines the very people who will be the protagonists of one of the most dramatic episodes in this true, yet untrue story about death and her vagaries. So there they stay. We forgot to say that the maiden aunt expressed one doubt, What will the neighbours say, she asked, when they notice the absence of these two people who were at death's door, but couldn't die. The maiden aunt does not usually speak in such a precious, roundabout way, but if she did so now it was in order not to break down in tears, which is what she would have done had she spoken the name of the child who had done no wrong in this world and the words, my brother. The father of the other three children said, We'll simply tell them what happened and await the consequences, we'll probably be accused of making secret burials, outside the cemetery and without the knowledge of the authorities, and, worse still, in another country, Well, let's just hope they don't start a war over it, said the aunt.

It was almost midnight when they set off for the frontier. The other villagers had taken longer than usual to retire to bed, as if they suspected that something strange was afoot. At last, silence reigned in the streets, and the lights in the houses gradually went out one by one. First, the mule was harnessed to the cart, then, with great difficulty even though he weighed so little, the grandfather was carried downstairs by his son-in-law and his two daughters, who reassured him when he asked faintly if they had the spade and the hoe with them, We do, don't worry, and then the mother went upstairs, took the child in her arms and said, Goodbye, my child, I'll never see you again, although this wasn't true, because she, too, would go in the cart with her sister and her brother-in-law, because they would need at least three people for the task ahead. The maiden aunt chose not to say goodbye to the travellers who would never return and, instead, shut herself up in the bedroom with her nephews. Since the metal rims of the cartwheels would make a terrible noise on the uneven surface of the road, with the grave risk of bringing curious householders to their windows to find out where their neighbours were going at that hour, they made a diversion along dirt tracks that finally brought them out onto the road beyond the village. They weren't very far from the frontier, but the trouble was that the road would not take them there, at a certain point they would have to leave it and continue along paths where the cart would barely fit, and the very last section would have to be made on foot, through the undergrowth, somehow or other carrying the grandfather. Fortunately, the son-in-law has a thorough knowledge of the area because, as well as having tramped these paths as a hunter, he had also made occasional use of them in his role as amateur smuggler. It took them almost two hours to reach the point where they would have to abandon the cart, and it was then that the son-in-law had the idea of putting the grandfather on the mule's back, trusting to the animal's sturdy legs. They unhitched the beast, removed any superfluous bits of harness, and then struggled to lift the old man up. The two women were crying, Oh, my poor father, Oh, my poor father, and their tears took from them what little strength they still had. The poor man was only semi-conscious, as if he were already crossing the first threshold of death. We can't do it, exclaimed the son-in-law in despair, then, suddenly, it occurred to him that the solution would be for him to get on the mule first and then pull the old man up afterwards onto the withers of the mule, I'll have to ride with my arms around him, there's no other way, you can help from down there. The child's mother went over to the cart to make sure he was still covered by the blanket, she didn't want the poor little thing to catch cold, and then she went back to help her sister, One, two, three, they said, but nothing happened, the body seemed to weigh like lead now, they could barely lift him off the ground. Then something extraordinary happened, a kind of miracle, a prodigy, a marvel. As if for a moment the law of gravity had been suspended or had begun to work in reverse, pushing up not down, the grandfather glided gently from his daughters' hands and, of his own accord, levitated his way into his son-in-law's open arms. The sky, which, since the onset of night had been covered by heavy, threatening clouds, cleared suddenly to reveal the moon. We can go on now, said the son-in-law, speaking to his wife, you lead the mule. The mother of the child drew back the blanket a little to look at her son. His closed eyelids were like two small, pale smudges, his face a blur. Then she let out a scream that pierced the air all around and made the beasts in their lairs tremble, I won't be the one to take my child to the other side, I didn't bring him into this world in order to hand him over to death, you take papa, I'll stay here. Her sister came over to her and asked, Would you rather watch him dying year by year, That's easy enough for you to say, you have three healthy children, But I care for your son as if he were my own, In that case, you take him, because I can't, And I shouldn't, because that would be like killing him, What's the difference, Taking someone to their death and killing them are two different things, you're the child's mother, not me, Would you be capable of taking one of your own children, or all of them, Yes, I think so, but I couldn't swear to it, Then I'm in the right, If that's what you want, then wait for us here, we're going to take papa. The sister went over to the mule, grasped the bridle and said, Shall we go, and her husband answered, Yes, but very slowly, I don't want him to slip off. The full moon was shining. Somewhere up ahead lay the frontier, that line which is only visible on maps. How will we know when we get there, asked the woman, Papa will know. She understood and asked no further questions. They continued on, another hundred yards, another ten steps, and suddenly the man said, We've arrived, Is it over, Yes. Behind them a voice repeated, It's over. The child's mother was for the last time clasping her dead son to her with her left arm, for resting on her right shoulder were the spade and hoe that the others had forgotten. Let's go a little further, as far as that ash tree, said the brother-in-law. Far off, on a hill, they could make out the lights of a village. From the way the mule was placing its feet, they could tell that the earth there was soft and would be easy to dig. This looks like a good place, said the man, the tree will serve as a marker when we come here to bring them flowers. The child's mother dropped the spade and hoe and tenderly laid her son on the ground. Then the two sisters, taking every care not to slip, received the body of their father and, without waiting for any help from the man who was now getting off the mule, they took the body and placed it beside that of his grandson. The child's mother was sobbing and repeating over and over, My son, my father, and her sister came and embraced her, weeping and saying, It's better like this, it's better like this, the life these poor unfortunates were living was no life at all. They both knelt down on the ground to mourn the dead who had come there to deceive death. The man was already working with the hoe, then he shifted the loosened earth with the spade and started digging again. The earth underneath was harder, more compacted, rather stony, and it took half an hour of solid work before the grave was deep enough. There was no coffin and no shroud, the bodies would rest on the bare earth, just with the clothes they had on. The man and the two women joined forces, with him standing in the grave and them above, and they managed, by degrees, to lower the old man's body into the hole, the women holding him by his outstretched arms, the man taking the weight until the body touched bottom. The women wept constantly, and although the man's eyes were dry, he was trembling all over, as if in the grip of a fever. The worst was yet to come. Amidst tears and sobs, the child was handed down and placed beside his grandfather, but he looked wrong there, a small, insignificant bundle, an unimportant life, left to one side as if he didn't belong to the family. Then the man bent over, picked up the child, lay him face down on his grandfather's chest, and arranged the grandfather's arms so that they were holding the tiny body, now they're comfortable, ready for their rest, we can start covering them with earth, careful now, just a little at a time, that way they can say their goodbyes to us, listen to what they're saying, goodbye my daughters, goodbye my son-in-law, goodbye my aunts and uncles, goodbye my mother. When the grave was filled, the man trod the earth down and smoothed it to make sure that no chance passer-by would notice that anyone was buried there. He placed a stone at the head and a smaller stone at the foot, then with the hoe he scattered over the grave the weeds he'd removed earlier, other living plants would soon take the place of those withered, dry, dead weeds, which would gradually enter the food cycle of the same earth from which they had sprung. The man paced out the distance between tree and grave, twelve paces, then he put the spade and hoe on his shoulder and said, Let's go. The moon had disappeared, the sky had once more clouded over. Just as they had finished hitching the mule to the cart, it started to rain.

THE PROTAGONISTS OF THESE DRAMATIC EVENTS, DESCRIBED IN unusually detailed fashion in a story which has, so far, preferred to offer the curious reader, if we may put it so, a panoramic view of the facts, were, when they unexpectedly entered the scene, given the social classification of poor country folk. This mistake, the result of an overhasty judgement on the part of the narrator, based on an assessment which was, at best, superficial, should, out of respect for the truth, be rectified at once. A family of poor country folk, if they were truly poor, would not be the owners of a cart nor would they have money enough to feed an animal with the large appetite of a mule. They were, in fact, a family of smallholders, reasonably well-off in the modest world they lived in, well-brought-up people with sufficient schooling to be able to hold conversations which were not only grammatically correct, but which also had what some, for lack of a better word, call content, others substance, and others, perhaps more vulgarly, meat. Were that not the case, the maiden aunt would never have been able to come out with the lovely sentence we commented on before, What will the neighbours say when they notice the absence of these two people who were at death's door, but couldn't die. Hurriedly filling in that gap, and with truth restored to its rightful place, let us now hear what the neighbours did say. Despite all the family's precautions, someone had seen the cart and puzzled over why those three people would be going out at that late hour. This was precisely the question the vigilant neighbour asked himself, Where are those three off to at this hour, a question repeated the following morning, with only slight modification, to the old farmer's son-in-law, Where were you three off to at that hour of the night. The son-in-law replied that they'd had some business to attend to, but the neighbour was not convinced, Business to attend to at midnight, with the cart, and your wife and your sister-in-law, that's a bit odd, isn't it, he said, It might be odd, but that's how it was, And where were you coming from when the sky was just beginning to grow light, That's hardly your affair, You're right, I'm sorry, it really isn't my affair, but I assume you won't mind my asking after your father-in-law, Much the same, And your little nephew, He's much the same too, Well, I hope they both get better, Thank you, Goodbye, Goodbye. The neighbour walked away, stopped and turned back, It seemed to me that you were carrying something in the cart, it seemed to me that your sister had a child in her arms, and if so, the figure lying down covered by a blanket was probably your father-in-law, what's more, What's more, what, What's more, when you came back, the cart was empty and your sister had no child in her arms, You obviously don't sleep much at night, No, I sleep very lightly and wake easily, You woke up when we left and when we came back, that's what people call coincidence, That's right, And you want me to tell you what happened, Only if you'd like to, Come with me. They went into the house, the neighbour greeted the three women, I don't wish to intrude, he said, embarrassed, and waited. You'll be the first person to know, said the son-in-law and you won't have to keep it a secret because we won't ask you to, Please, only tell me what you want to, My father-in-law and my nephew died last night, we took them over the border, where death is still active, You killed them, exclaimed the neighbour, In a way, yes, given that they couldn't have gone there under their own steam, but in a way, no, because we did it at the request of my father-in-law, and as for the child, poor thing, he had no voice in the matter and no life worth living, they're buried at the foot of an ash tree, in each other's arms you might say. The neighbour clutched his head, And now, Now you'll go and tell the whole village, we'll be arrested and taken to the police, and probably tried and sentenced for what we didn't do, But you did do it, A yard from the frontier they were still alive, a yard further on, they were dead, when exactly, according to you, did we kill them and how, If you hadn't taken them there, Yes, they would be here, waiting for a death that wouldn't come. Silent and serene, the three women were watching the neighbour. I'm off, he said, I thought something had happened, but I never imagined anything like this, Please, I have a favour to ask, said the son-in-law, What, Come with me to the police, that way you won't have to go from door to door telling people about the horrible crimes we've committed, I mean, imagine, patricide and infanticide, good grief, what monsters live in this house, That isn't how I would put it, Yes, I know, so come with me, When, Now, strike while the iron is hot, Let's go then.

They were neither tried nor sentenced. Like a lit fuse, the news spread rapidly through the nation, the media inveighed against the loathsome creatures, the murderous sisters, the son-in-law accomplice, they shed tears over the old man and the innocent child as if they were the grandfather and grandson everyone would like to have had, for the thousandth time, those right-thinking newspapers who acted as barometers of public morality pointed the finger at the unstoppable decline in traditional family values, which was, in their opinion, the fount, cause and origin of all ills, and then, only forty-eight hours later, news started coming in of identical incidents happening throughout the border regions. Other carts and other mules transported other defenceless bodies, fake ambulances wound along deserted country lanes to reach the place where they could unload the bodies, usually kept in their seats for the duration by seat belts, although there was the occasional disgraceful instance of bodies being stowed in the boot and covered with a blanket, cars of all makes, models and prices journeyed towards this new guillotine, whose blade, if you'll forgive the very free comparison, was the slender line of the frontier invisible to the naked eye, each vehicle carrying those poor unfortunates whom death, on this side of the line, had kept in a state of permanent dying. Not all the families who acted thus could allege in their defence the same motives, in some ways respectable, but nevertheless debatable, as our anguished farming family who, never imagining the consequences of their actions, had sparked this traffic. Some who made use of this expedient to get rid of their father or grandfather in a foreign land merely saw it as a clean, efficient way, although radical might be a better word, of freeing themselves from the genuine dead-weights that their dying relatives had become to them at home. The media who, earlier, had energetically denounced the daughters and son-in-law of the old man buried along with his grandson, including in their vituperations the maiden aunt, accusing her of complicity and connivance, now stigmatised the cruelty and lack of patriotism of apparently decent folk who, at this time of grave national crisis, had let slip the hypocritical mask that concealed their true natures. Under pressure from the governments of the three neighbouring countries and from the opposition parties, the prime minister condemned these inhumane activities, citing the need to respect human life and announcing that the armed forces would immediately take up positions along the frontier to prevent any citizen in a state of terminal physical decline from crossing over, whether on their own initiative or due to some arbitrary decision taken by relatives. Deep down, of course, although the prime minister dared not say this out loud, the government was not entirely opposed to an exodus which would, in the final analysis, serve the interests of the country by helping to lower the demographic pressure that had been building continuously over the last three months, although it was still far from reaching truly worrying levels. The prime minister also neglected to say that he'd had a discreet meeting with the interior minister that very day, the aim of which was to set up a nationwide network of vigilantes, or spies, in cities, towns and villages, whose mission would be to inform the authorities of any suspicious moves made by people with close relatives in a state of suspended death. The decision to intervene or not would be made on a case-by-case basis, since it was not the government's intention to put a complete stop to this new kind of migratory urge, but, rather, to satisfy, at least in part, the concerns of the governments of countries with whom they shared a border, enough, at least, to silence their complaints for a time. We're not here just to do what they want us to do, said the prime minister firmly, The plan will still exclude small hamlets, large estates and isolated houses, remarked the interior minister, We'll leave them to their own devices, they can do what they like, for as you know from experience, my friend, it's impossible to have one policeman per person.

For two weeks, the plan worked more or less perfectly, but, after that, some of the vigilantes started complaining that they were receiving threatening phone calls, warning them that, if they wanted to live a nice quiet life, they had better turn a blind eye to the clandestine traffic of the terminally ill, and even close their eyes completely if they didn't want to add their own corpse to the number of people with whose surveillance they had been charged. These were not empty threats, as became clear when the families of four vigilantes were told by anonymous callers that they should pick their loved ones up at such and such a place. And there they were, not dead, but not alive either. Given the gravity of the situation, the interior minister decided to show his power to the unknown enemy, on the one hand, by ordering his spies to intensify their investigations, and, on the other, by cancelling the drip-drip system of letting this one through, but not that one, which had been applied in accordance with the prime minister's tactics. The response was immediate, four more vigilantes suffered the same sad fate as the previous four, but, in this case, there was only one telephone call, intended for the interior minister himself, which could be interpreted as a provocation, but also as an action determined by pure logic, like someone saying, We exist. The message, however, did not stop there, it brought with it a constructive proposal, Let's come to a gentlemen's agreement, said the voice on the other end, you order your vigilantes to withdraw and we'll take charge of discreetly transporting the dying to the border, Who are you, asked the department head who answered the call, Just a group of people who care about order and discipline, all of us highly competent in our field, people who hate confusion and always keep our promises, in short, we're honest folk, And does this group have a name, asked the civil servant, Some call us the maphia, with a ph, Why the ph, To distinguish us from the original mafia, The state doesn't make agreements with mafias, Not on documents signed by a notary, no, Nor on any others, What position do you hold, Department head, That is, someone who knows nothing about real life, But I know my responsibilities, All that interests us at the moment is that you present our proposal to the person in authority, to the minister, if you have access to him, No, I don't have access to the minister, but this conversation will be passed on immediately to my superiors, The government will have forty-eight hours to study the proposal, not a minute more, but warn your superiors that if we don't get the answer we want, there will be more vigilantes in a state of coma, Right, I'll do that, So I'll phone again the day after tomorrow at the same time to find out what their decision is, Fine, I'll make a note, It's been a pleasure talking to you, If only I could say the same, Oh, I'm sure you'll change your tune when you hear that the vigilantes have returned home safe and sound, and if you haven't yet forgotten your childhood prayers, start praying now that they do just that, I understand, I knew you would, Right then, Forty-eight hours and not a minute more, But I certainly won't be the person who speaks to you, Oh, I'm certain you will be, Why's that, Because the minister won't want to speak to me directly, besides, if things go wrong, you'll be the one to carry the can, after all, what we're proposing is a gentlemen's agreement, Yes, sir, Goodbye, Goodbye. The department head removed the tape from the tape-recorder and went to speak to his immediate superior.

Half an hour later, the cassette was in the hands of the interior minister. He listened, listened again, listened a third time and then asked, Is this department head to be trusted, Well, replied the superior, up until now I've never had the slightest reason for complaint, Nor the greatest, I hope, Neither great nor small, said the superior, who had failed to catch the irony. The minister removed the cassette from the tape-player and started unravelling the tape. When he had finished, he placed it in a large glass ashtray and held the flame of his lighter to it. The tape began to wrinkle and crumple, and in less than a minute was transformed into a shapeless, blackened, fragile tangle. They probably recorded the conversation with the department head too, said the superior, That doesn't matter, anyone can fake a phone conversation, all you need are two voices and a tape-recorder, what matters is that we've destroyed our tape, and burning the original means burning any potential copies too, Needless to say the telephone operator keeps a record of all phone-calls, We'll make sure that disappears too, shall we, Yes, sir, and now, if I may, I'll leave you to consider the matter, No need, I've already come up with a response, That hardly surprises me, minister, given that you are lucky enough to be a very quick thinker, That would be mere flattery if it didn't happen to be true, because I do think quickly, Are you going to accept the proposal, No, I'm going to make a counter-proposal, They may, I'm afraid, reject it, the terms in which the emissary spoke were both peremptory and threatening, if we don't get the answer we want, there will be more vigilantes in a state of coma, those were his words, My dear fellow, the answer we're going to give them is precisely the answer they're expecting, Sorry, sir, I don't understand, That, my dear fellow, is your problem, and I don't wish to wound your feelings when I say this, but your problem is that you're not capable of thinking like a minister, My fault entirely, Oh, please, don't blame yourself, if you're ever called upon to serve the country as a minister, you'll see how your brain leaps the moment you sit down in a chair like this, the difference is quite unimaginable, Yes, but I'm a mere civil servant and will gain nothing by nurturing fantasies like that, You know the old saying, never say from this water I will not drink, Right now, sir, you have some very bitter water indeed to drink, said the superior, indicating the burned remains of the tape, When you follow a clear-cut strategy and know all the facts of the matter, it's not so very hard to draw up a safe plan of action, I'm all ears, minister, The day after tomorrow, given that your department head will be the one to speak to the emissary, he and no one else will be the ministry's negotiator and he'll tell them that we agree to examine the proposal they made to us, but will warn them, too, that public opinion and the opposition party would never allow all those thousands of vigilantes to be withdrawn from service without some reasonable explanation, And, obviously, to say that the maphia have taken over the running of the business would hardly be thought a reasonable explanation, Precisely, although you could perhaps have put it a little more diplomatically, Forgive me, minister, it just came out like that, Anyway, at that point, the department head will present a counter-proposal, or what we might also call an alternative suggestion, namely, that the vigilantes will not be withdrawn from service, they will remain where they are now, but deactivated, Deactivated, Yes, the word is clear enough, I think, Oh, indeed, minister, I was merely expressing my surprise, Surprise about what, after all, it's the only way we have of not appearing to be giving in to the rascals' blackmail, Even though we have, The important thing is that it doesn't look as if we have, that we preserve the façade, what happens behind that façade will no longer be our responsibility, Meaning, Let's just imagine that we intercept a vehicle and arrest the men in charge of it, needless to say those risks were included in the bill that the relatives had to pay, There won't be any bills or receipts, the maphia don't pay taxes, That's just a manner of speaking, what matters is the fact that it's a win-win situation for everyone, for us because it's a load off our minds, for the vigilantes because they will no longer run the risk of suffering any physical harm, for the families because they can rest easy knowing that their living-dead will finally be transformed into their dead, and for the maphia because they'll get paid for their work, A perfect arrangement, minister, One that comes with the cast-iron guarantee that it will be to no one's advantage to blab, No, you're probably right, Perhaps I seem a little too cynical, Not at all, minister, I only admire the way in which you came up with such a solid, logical, coherent plan, Experience, my friend, experience, Right, I'll go and talk to the department head and pass your instructions on to him, I'm sure he'll give a good acount of himself, because as I said before, he's never given me the slightest reason for complaint, Nor the largest, I believe, Neither one nor the other, replied the superior, who had finally understood the little joke.

Everything or, to be more exact, almost everything went as the minister had foreseen. At precisely the hour agreed, not a minute before, not a minute afterwards, the emissary from the criminal association, the self-styled maphia, phoned to hear what the ministry had to say. The department head deserved full marks for the way in which he carried out his role, he was firm and clear and persuasive as regards the fundamental question, namely, that the vigilantes, albeit deactivated, would remain at their posts, and he had the satisfaction of receiving in return, and of being able to pass on to his superior, the best of all possible replies in the circumstances, that the government's alternative suggestion would be examined closely and that another phone call would ensue in twenty-four hours' time. And that is what happened. The close examination concluded that the government's proposal could be accepted, but with one condition, that the only vigilantes to be deactivated should be those who had remained loyal to the government, or, in other words, those whom the maphia had failed to persuade to collaborate with the new boss, that is, the maphia itself. Let us try to understand the criminals' point of view. Faced by a long, complex operation on a national scale, and having to employ many of their more experienced personnel in visiting those families who would, in principle at least, be prepared to rid themselves of their loved ones for the praiseworthy reason that they wished to spare them not only pointless, but eternal suffering, it would clearly be a great help to the maphia if they could make use of the government's vast network of informers, with the added convenience that it allowed them to continue using their preferred weapons of corruption, bribery and intimidation. It was against this stone, suddenly thrown into the middle of the road, that the interior minister's strategy stubbed its toe, causing serious damage to the dignity of state and government. Caught between a rock and a hard place, between scylla and charybdis, between the devil and the deep blue sea, he rushed to consult the prime minister about this unexpected gordian knot. The worst of it was that things had gone too far for them to be able to turn back now. The prime minister, despite being more experienced than the interior minister, could find no better way out of the difficulty than to propose further negotiations, establishing a kind of numerus clausus, with something like a maximum of twenty-five per cent of the total number of current vigilantes going over to work for the other side. Once again it would fall to the department head to transmit to his now impatient interlocutor the conciliatory platform which the prime minister and the interior minister, ever-hopeful, believed would finally allow the agreement to be ratified. It would, however, be an agreement with no signatures, since it was a gentlemen's agreement, in which one's word was enough, thus, as the dictionary explains, avoiding any legal formalities. They clearly had no idea what twisted, evil minds the maphiosi have. Firstly, the maphia gave no deadline for a response, leaving the poor interior minister on tenterhooks and convinced now that he would be obliged to hand in his letter of resignation. Secondly, when, after several days, it occurred to them that they really should phone, it was only to say that they had still not reached a conclusion as to whether or not the platform would prove sufficiently conciliatory, and then, in passing, as if it were a matter of no importance, they took the opportunity to inform them that they were not in any way responsible for the fact that, the previous day, four more vigilantes had been found in a desperate state of health. Thirdly, because everything has an ending, be it happy or not, the answer that had just been given to the government by the national maphioso board, via the department head and his superior, was divided into two points, point a, the numerus clausus would be not twenty-five per cent, but thirty-five, point b, whenever they felt it suited their interests, and with no need for prior consultation with the authorities, far less their consent, the organisation demanded that it be given the right to transfer the vigilantes working for them to posts occupied by deactivated vigilantes, whom they would, of course, replace. Take it or leave it. Do you see any way out of this dilemma, the prime minister asked the interior minister, Well, sir, I'm not even sure it exists, if we refuse, I estimate that every day we'll have four vigilantes rendered useless both for work and life, if we accept, we'll be in the hands of these people for who knows how long, For ever, or for at least as long as there are families who want to rid themselves at whatever price of the burdens they have at home, That's just given me an idea, I'm not sure whether to be pleased to hear that or not, Look, I've done the best I can, prime minister, but if I've become another kind of burden, then you just have to say the word, Oh, don't be so sensitive, come on, what's this idea of yours, Well, prime minister, I believe we're faced here by a clear case of supply and demand, What's that got to do with anything, we're talking here about people who have only one way to die, As with the classic question about which came first, the chicken or the egg, it's not always easy to tell whether the demand preceded the supply or if, on the contrary, it was the supply that created the demand, Perhaps I should consider moving you from the ministry of the interior to the finance department, They're not so very different, prime minister, the ministry of the interior has its finances, and the finance department has its interior, they're communicating vessels, so to speak, Stick to the point and tell me your idea, If it hadn't occurred to that first family that the solution to the problem might be waiting for them on the other side of the border, the situation in which we find ourselves today would perhaps be different, if a lot of families hadn't followed their example, the maphia wouldn't have turned up, wanting to exploit a business that simply didn't exist, In theory, yes, although, as we know, they're perfectly capable of squeezing water out of a stone and then selling it on for a profit, so I'm afraid I still don't see what your idea is, It's simple, prime minister, If only it were, Put briefly, we have to turn off the supply, And how would we do that, By persuading families, in the name of the most sacred principles of humanity, love for one's neighbour and solidarity, to keep their terminally ill loved ones at home, And how exactly do you think such a miracle would happen, My idea is to run a massive publicity campaign in all the media, press, television and radio, including street parades, consciousness-raising groups, the distribution of pamphlets and stickers, street theatre and straight theatre, films, especially sentimental dramas and cartoons, a campaign capable of moving people to tears, a campaign that would cause relatives who have strayed from their duties and obligations to repent, one that would awaken in people feelings of solidarity, self-sacrifice and compassion, it would, I'm convinced, take only a short time for the guilty families to become aware of the unforgivable cruelty of their actions and to return to the transcendent values which not so very long ago formed their bedrock, My doubts are growing by the minute, now I'm wondering if I shouldn't move you to culture, or perhaps religion, for which you also seem to have a certain vocation, Or else, prime minister, place the three portfolios under one ministry, You mean as well as the finance department, Well, yes, if they really are communicating vessels, What you wouldn't be suited to at all, my friend, would be propaganda, your idea that a publicity campaign would bring families back into the fold of sensitive souls is utter nonsense, Why, prime minister, Because campaigns like that only profit those who earn money making them, We've done plenty of such campaigns before, Yes, and you've seen the results, besides, to go back to the matter that should be concerning us, even if your campaign were to bear fruit, it wouldn't do so today or tomorrow, and I have to make a decision now, Indeed, prime minister. The prime minister gave a despairing smile, This whole thing is ridiculous, absurd, he said, we know very well that we have no choice and that any proposals we make will only serve to make the situation worse, In that case, In that case, and if we don't want to have on our conscience four vigilantes a day battered to within an inch of their lives and left at death's door, all we can do is to accept their conditions, We could order a lightning strike by the police, a surprise attack, and arrest dozens of maphiosi, that might make them take a step back, The only way to kill the dragon is by cutting off its head, clipping its nails will have no effect at all, It might help, Four vigilantes a day, minister, remember that, four vigilantes a day, it's best if we recognise that we're tied hand and foot, The opposition will have a field day, they'll accuse us of selling the country to the maphia, They won't say country, they'll say nation, Even worse, Let's just hope the church is willing to help, after all, I imagine they'll be receptive to the argument that, as well as providing them with a few useful deaths, the reason we made this decision was to save lives, You can't talk about saving lives any more, prime minister, that was before, You're right, we'll have to come up with some other expression. There was a silence. Then the prime minister said, Enough of this, give the necessary instructions to your department head and start work on the deactivation plan, we also need to know the maphia's thinking on how to distribute the twenty-five per cent of vigilantes who will make up the numerus clausus, Thirty-five per cent, prime minister, Please don't remind me that our defeat has been even worse than we at first thought, It's a sad day, If the families of the next four vigilantes knew what was going on here, they wouldn't say so, And to think that those four vigilantes might be working for the maphia tomorrow, That's life, my dear head of the ministry of communicating vessels, Ministry of the interior, prime minister, of the interior, Oh, that's just the tube that connects all the other tubes together.

YOU MIGHT THINK THAT AFTER ALL THE SHAMEFUL CAPITULATIONS made by the government during the ups and downs of their negotiations with the maphia, going so far as to allow humble, honest public servants to begin working full-time for that criminal organisation, you might think that, morally speaking, they could sink no lower. Alas, when one advances blindly across the boggy ground of realpolitik, when pragmatism takes up the baton and conducts the orchestra, ignoring what is written in the score, you can be pretty sure that, as the imperative logic of dishonour will show, there are still, after all, a few more steps to descend. Through the relevant ministry, that of defence, known, in more honest times, as the ministry of war, orders were issued to the troops positioned along the frontier to limit themselves to guarding only the A-roads, especially those that led into the neighbouring countries, leaving all B- and C-roads to wallow in bucolic peace, along with, and this for very good reasons, the complex network of local roads, lanes, footpaths, tracks and shortcuts. This, inevitably, meant a return to barracks for most of the troops, which, while it gladdened the hearts of the rank and file, including corporals and quartermasters, who were all thoroughly fed up with guard duty and patrols day and night, caused, on the other hand, great feelings of discontent amongst the sergeants, apparently more aware than the others of the importance of the values of military honour and service to the nation. Now if the capillary movement of that displeasure reached as far as the second lieutenants and lost some of its impetus when it got to the first lieutenants, the truth is that it redoubled in strength when it reached the level of the captains. Naturally, none of them would dare to pronounce out loud the dangerous word maphia, but, when they talked about it among themselves, they could not help but recall how in the days prior to their return to barracks they had intercepted a number of vans transporting terminally ill patients and that beside each driver there had sat an officially accredited vigilante who, without even being asked, had produced, with all the necessary stamps, signatures and seals, a piece of paper which, for reasons of national interest, gave express authorisation for the transportation of the ailing Mr or Mrs so-and-so to some unspecified destination, and stated that the army should feel obliged to give all the assistance they could in order to ensure the occupants of each van a safe and successful journey. None of this would have provoked any doubts in the minds of the worthy sergeants had it not been for a strange coincidence, for on at least seven occasions, the vigilante had handed the soldier the document to be checked and given him a knowing wink. Considering the geographical distance between the places in which these episodes of country life had occurred, the sergeants immediately dismissed the hypothesis that it might have been, shall we say, an equivocal gesture, a rather primitive come-on in a game of seduction between persons of the same sex or, indeed, although in this case it hardly mattered, of different sexes. However, it was the vigilantes' evident nervousness, more pronounced in some than in others it's true, but all of whom behaved as if they were throwing a bottle into the sea with a message inside it calling for help, that led the sharp-eyed corps of sergeants to think that inside these vans skulked that most famous of cats which, when it wants to be discovered, always finds a way to leave the tip of its tail showing. Then came the inexplicable order to return to barracks, followed by a few whispered rumours, which arose who knows how or where, but which some purveyors of news hinted, in confidence, might have come from the interior minister himself. The opposition newspapers spoke of the unhealthy atmosphere being breathed in the barracks, while newspapers close to the government vehemently denied that such miasmas were poisoning the esprit de corps of the armed forces, but the fact is that rumours of a possible military coup, although no one could explain the supposed reasons for such a coup, spread everywhere and, for the moment, forced onto the back-burner of public interest the problem of the sick who were unable to die. Not that the problem had been forgotten, as was proved by a phrase in circulation at the time and much repeated by the denizens of cafés, Even if there is a military coup, at least we can be sure of one thing, however many shots they fire at each other, they won't succeed in killing anyone. Everyone expected, at any moment, a dramatic appeal from the king for national unity, a communiqué from the government announcing a package of urgent measures, a statement from the high commands of the army and the airforce, but not the navy, unnecessary in a landlocked country, protesting their absolute loyalty to the legitimately constituted powers, a manifesto from writers, a stance taken by artists, a concert in solidarity, an exhibition of revolutionary posters, a general strike called by the two main trade unions, a pastoral letter from the bishops urging prayer and fasting, a procession of penitents, a mass distribution of pamphlets, yellow, blue, green, red, white, there was even talk of a mass demonstration whose participants would be the thousands of people of all ages and conditions who found themselves in a state of suspended death, parading down the main avenues of the capital on stretchers, in wheelbarrows, in ambulances, or on the backs of their more robust children, with, at the front of the cortège, a huge banner that said, sacrificing a few commas to make the couplet work, We here who cannot die await all of you who pass us by. In the end, none of this proved necessary. It's true that suspicions of the maphia's direct involvement in the transportation of the dying did not go away, it's true that that these were even reinforced in the light of subsequent events, but a single hour was all it took for a sudden threat from the enemy-without to calm the fratricidal mood and prompt the three estates, church, nobility and people, for despite the country's progressive ideas, the three estates still existed, to rally round their king and, with some justifiable reluctance, round the government too. The facts, as tends to be the case, can be told in few words.

Angered by the continual invasion of their territories by commandos of grave-diggers, either employed by the maphia or there of their own volition, coming from that aberrant land where no one died, and after various futile diplomatic protests, the governments of the three neighbouring countries decided, in a concerted action, to bring out their troops and protect their frontiers, with strict orders to shoot after the third warning. It's worth mentioning that the deaths of a few maphiosi shot down at almost point-blank range after crossing the line of separation, something we usually refer to as an occupational hazard, was immediately used as an excuse for the organisation, in the name of personal safety and operational risks, to increase the prices on its list of services offered. Having mentioned this interesting little sidelight on the workings of the maphia's administration, let us move on to what really matters. Once again, using a tactically impeccable manoeuvre to circumvent the ditherings of the government and the doubts of the armed forces' high commands, the sergeants seized the initiative and became, in everyone's eyes, the promoters, and consequently also the heroes, of the popular protest movement that marched forth to demand, en masse, in squares, avenues and streets, the immediate return of the troops to the battle front. Indifferent to and untouched by the terrible problems faced by the country on this side of the border, struggling, as it was, with its quadruple crisis, demographic, social, political and economic, the countries on the other side had finally dropped their mask and revealed to the light of day their true face, that of harsh conquistadors and implacable imperialists. In shops and homes, on the radio, on the television and in the newspapers, what one heard and read was, They're jealous of us, they're envious of the fact that no one here dies, that's why they want to invade and occupy our territory so that they won't have to die either. After two days, marching flat out and with flags flying, singing patriotic songs like the marseillaise, ça ira, maria da fonte, the hino da carta, não verás país nenhum, the red flag, the portuguesa, god save the king, the internationale, deutschland über alles, the chant des marais, and the stars and stripes, the soldiers returned to the posts they had left, and there, armed to the teeth, waited staunchly for imminent attack and for glory. There was neither. Neither glory nor attack. There were few conquests and even less empire-building, for the aforementioned neighbouring countries simply wanted to stop this new species of forced migrant being buried there without due authorisation, and it wouldn't be so bad if all they did was bury them, but they brought them there to be killed, murdered, eliminated, finished off, since it was at the precise, fateful moment when they crossed the frontier, feet first so that the head would be aware of what was happening to the rest of the body, that the poor unfortunates passed away, uttered their last sigh. The two valiant camps faced each other, but the rivers will not run red with blood this time either. This had nothing to do with the men on this side of the border, for they knew they wouldn't die even if a burst of machine-gun fire cut them in two. Although, out of perfectly legitimate scientific curiosity, we should ask ourselves how the two halves could survive in cases where the stomach was left on one side and the intestines on the other. Whatever the truth of the matter, only a complete madman would have considered firing the first shot. And, thank god, it never was fired. Indeed, the only consequence of a few soldiers from the other side deciding to desert to the eldorado where no one dies was that they were sent straight back where they came from and where a court martial awaited them. This fact is entirely irrelevant to the narrative of the complicated story we've been telling and we will not speak of it again, but neither did we want merely to relegate it to the darkness of the inkwell. The court martial will probably decide a priori not to take account in their deliberations of the ingenuous desire for eternal life that has always inhabited the human heart, What would happen if we all lived for ever, where would it end, the prosecution will ask, resorting to the lowest of rhetorical blows, and the defence, needless to say, won't have wit enough to come up with a fitting answer, for they have no idea where it will end either. Let us only hope that they do not shoot the poor devils. Then it really could be said that they went out for wool and came home shorn.

Let's change the subject. When we mentioned the suspicions harboured by the sergeants, and by their allies amongst certain second lieutenants and captains, about the maphia's direct involvement in the transportation of the dying to the border, we said that these suspicions were strengthened by certain subsequent events. The moment has come to reveal what those were and how they came about. Taking as their example the family of smallholders who began the whole process, what the maphia have been doing is simply crossing the border, burying the dead, and charging a small fortune for the service. With the difference that they paid no attention to the beauty of the site and never bothered to note down in their log-book any orographic or topographic reference points that might, in future, help tearful family members, repenting of their evil deeds, to find the grave again and beg forgiveness of the dead. One doesn't require a strategically acute mind to understand that the armies ranged along the other side of the three frontiers had begun to constitute a serious obstacle to funerary practices which had, up until then, taken place unobstructed. The maphia would not be what it is had it failed to find a solution to the problem. It really is a shame, if you will allow us a brief aside, that the brilliant intellects leading these criminal organisations should have departed from the strait and narrow path of respect for the law and disobeyed the wise biblical precept that urges us to earn our daily bread by the sweat of our brow, but facts are facts, and while repeating adamastor's sad words, ah, but my heart is sick to tell the tale, we will set down here the distressing news of the trick deployed by the maphia to get round a difficulty which was, to all appearances, insoluble. Before doing so, however, it might be as well to explain that the word sick, placed by the epic poet in the mouth of the unhappy giant adamastor, meant, in that context, profoundly sad, sorrowful, griefstricken, but for some years now, ordinary people have thought, and quite rightly too, that they could make use of that excellent word to express feelings of disgust, repugnance, loathing, which, as anyone will recognise, have nothing to do with the feelings described above. One cannot be too careful with words, they change their minds just as people do. Obviously, the trick wasn't as simple as making sausages, stuff 'em, tie 'em up and stick 'em in the smokeroom, the matter took time, it required emissaries with false moustaches and hats with the brim low over their eyes, telegrams in code, conversations down secret phone lines, on red telephones, midnight meetings at crossroads, notes left under stones, all of which elements we had noted in the earlier negotiations, when, so to speak, they were playing at dice with the lives of the vigilantes. Nor must one think that these transactions were, as in the earlier case, purely bilateral. As well as the maphia in this country where no one dies, the maphias in the neighbouring countries also took part in these talks, for that was the only way to protect both the independence of each criminal organisation within the national framework in which it worked and the independence of their respective governments. It would be completely unacceptable, absolutely reprehensible for the maphia in one of those countries to negotiate directly with the administration of another. Things, however, did not reach that point, having been prevented from doing so up until now, as if by a last vestige of modesty, by the sacrosanct principle of national sovereignty, a principle as important to maphias as it is to governments, and while this is perfectly understandable in the latter, you might have your doubts when it came to criminal associations, until you remembered with what jealous brutality they defended their territories from the hegemonic ambitions of their professional colleagues. Coordinating all this, bringing together the general and the particular, balancing the interests of some with the interests of others, was not an easy task, which explains why, for two long, boring weeks of waiting, the soldiers had passed the time insulting each other over the loudspeakers, although always taking care not to overstep the mark, not to be too rude, in case the offence should go to the head of some particularly prickly lieutenant-colonel and then all hell would break loose. The biggest contributing factor in complicating and delaying the negotiations was the fact that none of the maphias in the other countries had teams of biddable vigilantes, and they therefore lacked the irresistible means of putting pressure on the government that had produced such excellent results here.

Although this darker side of the negotiations has never been revealed, except in the form of the inevitable rumours, there are good reasons for thinking that the middle-ranking commanders of the armies in the neighbouring countries, with the indulgent approval of their superior officers, had allowed themselves to be persuaded, god alone knows at what price, by the arguments of the local maphia spokesmen, to close their eyes to the unavoidable comings and goings, advances and retreats, in which the solution to the problem consisted. A child could have come up with the idea, but to put it into practice, he would, having reached what we call the age of reason, have had to go and knock on the door of the maphia's recruiting section and say, My vocation has brought me here, do with me as you will.

Lovers of concision, laconicism and economy of language will doubtless be asking, if the idea is such a simple one, why did we need all this waffle to arrive, at last, at the critical point. The answer is equally simple, and we will give it using a current and very trendy term, that will, we hope, make up for the archaisms with which, in the likely opinion of some, we have spattered this account as if with mould, and that term is context. Now everyone knows what we mean by context, but there could have been doubts had we rather dully used that dreadful archaism background, which is, moreover, not entirely faithful to the truth, given that the context gives not only the background, but all the innumerable other grounds that exist between the subject observed and the line of the horizon. It would be better then if we called it a framework. Yes, a framework, and now that we finally have it well and truly framed, the moment has come to reveal the nature of the trick that the maphia thought up to avoid any chance of a conflict that might prejudice their interests. As we have said, a child could have come up with the idea. It was this, to take the sufferer across the frontier, and, once he or she had died, to bring him or her back to be buried in the maternal bosom of his country of origin. A perfect checkmate in the most rigorous, exact and precise meaning of the word. As we have seen, the problem was resolved without discredit to any of the parties, and the four armies, who now had no reason to remain at the frontier on a war footing, could withdraw peacefully, since the maphia proposed simply to enter and then leave again, for, as we have said before, the dying expired the moment they were transported to the other side, and now there will be no need for them to linger even for a minute, merely the time it takes to die, and that, which has always been the briefest of moments, just a sigh, that's all, so you can imagine how it would be in this case, a candle that suddenly burns itself out without anyone even having to blow. Not even the gentlest of euthanasias could be as easy or as sweet. The most interesting aspect of the new situation is that the justice system of the country in which people do not die finds itself without any legal basis on which to take action against the buriers, always supposing they really wanted to, and not just because of the gentlemen's agreement that the government was forced to make with the maphia. It can't accuse them of homicide because, technically speaking, no homicide takes place, and also because the reprehensible act, and if anyone can find a better way of describing it, then please do, takes place abroad, and they can't even accuse them of burying the dead, since that is the natural fate of the dead, and they should be grateful that there is someone prepared to take on a task which, however you look at it, is a painful one, both from the physical and the psychological viewpoint. They could, at most, allege that no doctor was present to record the death, that the burial did not fulfil the regulations set down for a correct interment and that, as if such a thing were quite unheard of, the grave is not only unmarked, but will certainly be lost from view once the first heavy rains come and the plants push up, tender and joyful, through the fertile soil. Having considered all the difficulties, and concerned that it might be plunged into the swamp of appeals in which, the maphia's clever lawyers, inveterate intriguers, would mercilessly drown them, the law decided to wait patiently to see how things turned out. This was, without a shadow of a doubt, the most prudent attitude to take. The country is in an unparalleled state of unrest, the powers-that-be are confused, authority undermined, moral values are rapidly being turned on their head, and a loss of any sense of civic respect is sweeping all sectors of society, probably even god has no idea where he's taking us. There is a rumour that the maphia is negotiating another gentlemen's agreement with the funeral industry in the hope of rationalising their efforts and spreading the workload, which means, in ordinary, everyday language, that they will supply the dead, and the undertakers will contribute the means and the technical expertise for burying them. It is also said that the maphia's proposal was welcomed with open arms by the undertakers, weary of wasting their millennia of knowledge, their experience, their know-how, and their choirs of professional mourners, on arranging funerals for dogs, cats and canaries, as well as the occasional cockatoo, a catatonic tortoise, a tame squirrel and a pet lizard whose owner used to carry it around on his shoulder. We have never sunk so low, they said. Now the future looked bright and cheerful, hopes bloomed like flowerbeds, indeed, one might even say, at the risk of the obvious paradox, that the funeral industry was reborn. And all thanks to the good offices and inexhaustible money vaults of the maphia. It provided subsidies to businesses in the capital and in other cities round the country for them to set up new branches, and the maphia was, of course, duly recompensed, in localities near the frontiers, it made arrangements for a doctor to be present when the dead person was brought back across the border and someone was required to declare them dead, and agreements were reached with local councils that the burials in the maphia's charge should have absolute priority, regardless of the hour of day or night when it chose to carry these out. Naturally, all of this cost a lot of money, but now that the extras and the supplementary services accounted for most of the bill, the business continued to be profitable. Then, without warning, the tap from which had flowed a constant, generous supply of the terminally dying was turned off. It seemed that families, suffering an attack of conscience, had passed the word from one to the other that they were no longer going to send their loved ones far away to die, that if, in the figurative sense, we had eaten of their flesh, then now we would have to gnaw on their bones as well, that we are not just here for the good times, when our loved ones had strength and health intact, we are here, too, for the bad times and the worst, when they have become little more than a stinking rag that there is no point in washing. The undertakers went from euphoria to despair, were thrown back into ruin and the humiliation of burying canaries and cats, dogs and the rest of the menagerie, the turtle, the cockatoo, the squirrel, but not the lizard because that had been the only one that let its owner carry it about on his shoulder. The maphia remained calm, kept their nerve, and immediately set out to investigate what was going on. It was quite simple. The families told them, although not always in so many words, that acting in secret had been one thing, with their loved ones carried off at dead of night, and when there was no way the neighbours could know if they were still lying racked on their bed of pain or had simply evaporated. It was easy to lie, to say sadly, Still here, poor thing, when you met your next-door neighbour on the landing and she asked, So how's grandpa these days. Now everything would be different, there would be a death certificate, there would be plaques in the cemeteries engraved with names and surnames, in a matter of hours the whole envious, slanderous neighbourhood would know that grandpa had died in the only way he could die, which meant, quite simply, that his own cruel, ungrateful family had despatched him to the frontier. It makes us feel ashamed, they confessed. The maphia listened and listened and said they would think about it. This took no more than twenty-four hours. Following the example of the old gentleman on page twenty-eight, the dead had wanted to die and their deaths would, therefore, be recorded on death certificates as suicides. The tap was turned on again.

IN THIS COUNTRY IN WHICH NO ONE DIES NOT EVERYTHING WAS as sordid as we have just described, nor, in this society torn between the hope of living for ever and the fear of never dying, did the voracious maphia succeed in getting its talons into every section by corrupting souls, subjugating bodies and besmirching the little that remained of the fine principles of old, when an envelope containing something that smelled of a bribe would have been immediately returned to the sender, bearing a firm and clear response, something along the lines of, Buy some toys for your children with this money, or You must have got the wrong address. Dignity was then a form of pride that was within the grasp of all classes. Despite every-thing, despite the false suicides and the dirty dealings on the frontier, that spirit continued to hover over the waters, not the waters of the great ocean sea, for that bathed other distant lands, but over lakes and rivers, over streams and brooks, over the puddles left by the rain, over the luminous depths of wells, which is where one can best judge how high the sky is, and, extraordinary though it may seem, over the calm surfaces of aquariums too. It was precisely when he was distractedly watching a goldfish that had just come up to the surface to breathe and when he was wondering, slightly less distractedly, just how long it had been since he changed the water, because he knew what the fish was trying to say when again and again it ruptured the delicate meniscus where water meets air, it was at precisely this revelatory moment that the apprentice philosopher was presented with the clear, stark question that would give rise to the most impassioned and thrilling controversy ever known in the whole history of this country where no one dies. This is what the spirit hovering over the water of the aquarium asked the apprentice philosopher, Have you ever wondered if death is the same for all living beings, be they animals, human beings included, or plants, from the grass you walk on to the hundred-metre-tall sequoiadendron giganteum, will the death that kills a man who knows he's going to die be the same as that of a horse who never will. And, it went on, at what point did the silkworm die after having shut itself up in the cocoon and bolted the door, how was it possible for the life of one to have been born out of the death of the other, the life of the moth out of the death of the worm, and for them to be the same but different, or did the silkworm not die because the moth still lives. The apprentice philosopher replied, The silkworm didn't die, but the moth will die after it has laid its eggs, Well, I knew that before you were born, said the spirit hovering over the waters of the aquarium, the silkworm didn't die, there was no corpse inside the cocoon when the moth had left, but, as you said, one was born out of the death of the other, It's called metamorphosis, everyone knows that, said the apprentice philosopher condescendingly, That's a very fine-sounding word, full of promises and certainties, you say metamorphosis and move on, it seems you don't understand that words are the labels we stick on things, not the things themselves, you'll never know what the things are really like, nor even what their real names are, because the names you gave them are just that, the names you gave them, Which of us is the philosopher, Neither you nor me, you're merely an apprentice philosopher, and I am merely the spirit hovering over the water in the aquarium, We were talking about death, No, not about death, about deaths, what I asked was why is it that human beings aren't dying, but other animals are, why is the non-death of some not also the non-death of others, when the life of this goldfish ends, and, I should warn you, that won't be long in coming if you don't change this water, would you be able to recognise in its death that other death from which at the moment, for reasons you don't know, you appear to be immune, Before, in the days when people died, on the few occasions when I found myself in the presence of people who had passed away, I never imagined that their death would be the same death I would one day die, Because each of you has his or her own death, you carry it with you in a secret place from the moment you're born, it belongs to you and you belong to it, And what about animals and plants, Well, I suppose it's the same with them, Each one with its own death, Exactly, So there are many deaths, as many as all the living beings that have existed, do exist and will exist, In a way, yes, You're contradicting yourself, exclaimed the apprentice philosopher, The deaths that oversee each individual are, so to speak, deaths with a limited life span, subaltern deaths, who die along with the thing they kill, but above them will be a larger death, the one that has been in charge of human beings since the dawn of the species, So there's a hierarchy, Yes, I suppose so, As there is for animals, from the most elementary protozoa to the blue whale, For them too, And for plants, from diatoms to the giant sequoia, which, because it's so big, you mentioned before with its latin name, As far as I know, the same thing happens with them, So each thing has its own personal, untransmittable death, Yes, And then two more general deaths, one for each of nature's kingdoms, Precisely, And is that where it ends, the hierarchy of responsibilities delegated by thanatos, asked the apprentice philosopher, If I go as far as my imagination can reach, I can see another death, the last, supreme death, What death is that, The one that will destroy the universe, the one that really deserves the name of death, although when that happens, there'll be no one around to pronounce its name, the other things we've been talking about are nothing but tiny, insignificant details, So there isn't just one death, concluded the apprentice philosopher somewhat unnecessarily, That's precisely what I've been saying, So the death that used to be our death has stopped working, but the others, the deaths of animals and plants, continue to operate, so they're independent, each working in their own sector, Now are you convinced, Yes, Right, now go and tell everyone else, said the spirit hovering over the water of the aquarium. And that is how the controversy started.

The first argument against the daring thesis proposed by the spirit hovering over the water of the aquarium was that its spokesperson was not a qualified philosopher, but a mere apprentice who had never gone beyond a few textbook rudiments, almost as elementary as the protozoa, and as if that were not enough, these rudiments had been taken from here, there and everywhere, in stray snippets, with no needle and thread to sew them together even though the colours and shapes clashed horribly, it was, in short, a philosophy that one might describe as being of the harlequin or eclectic school of thought. That wasn't really the problem, though. It's true that the essence of the thesis had been the work of the spirit hovering over the water of the aquarium, however, one need only re-read the dialogue on the two previous pages to recognise that the apprentice philosopher's contribution also had some influence on the gestation of this interesting idea, if only in his role as listener, a dialectical factor which, as everyone knows, has been indispensable ever since the days of socrates. There was one thing, at least, that could not be denied, human beings were not dying, but other animals were. As for the plants, anyone, however ignorant of botany, could easily see that, just as before, they were being born, putting out leaves, then withering and drying up entirely, and if that final phase, with or without putrefaction, could not be described as dying, then perhaps someone could step up and offer a better definition. The fact that the people here were not dying, but all other living things were, said some objectors, could only be seen as proof that normality had not entirely withdrawn from the world, and normality, needless to say, means, purely and simply, dying when our time comes. Dying and not getting caught up in arguments about whether that death was ours from birth, or if it was merely passing by and happened to notice us. In other countries, people continued to die, and the inhabitants didn't seem any unhappier for that. At first, as is only natural, there was envy, there were conspiracies, there was even the odd case of attempted scientific espionage to find out how we had managed it, but, when they saw the problems besetting us, we believe that the feeling among the populations of those countries could best be expressed in these words, We've had a very lucky escape.

The church, of course, galloped into the arena of the debate mounted on its usual war-horse, namely, that god moves, as always, in mysterious ways, which means, in layman's terms somewhat tinged with verbal impiety, that we cannot even peer through the crack in the door of heaven to see what's going on inside. The church also said that the temporary and more or less lasting suspension of natural causes and effects wasn't really a novelty, one had only to recall the infinite miracles that had happened over the last twenty centuries, the only difference, compared with what was happening now, was the sheer scale of the thing, for what was once bestowed as a favour on one individual, by the grace of his or her personal faith, had been replaced by a depersonalised, global gift, a whole country being given, so to speak, the elixir of eternal life, and not only the believers, who, as is only logical, might expect to be singled out, but also atheists, agnostics, heretics, apostates, unbelievers of every kind, devotees of other religions, the good, the bad and the worse, the virtuous and the maphiosi, executioners and victims, cops and robbers, murderers and blood donors, the mad and the sane, all, without exception, were at the same time witnesses and beneficiaries of the greatest marvel ever seen in the whole history of miracles, the eternal life of a body eternally bound to the eternal life of the soul. The catholic hierarchy, from the bishops up, were not amused by these mystical tales issuing from certain members of their middle ranks avid for wonders, and they let it be known in a very firm message to the faithful, in which, after the inevitable reference to god's impenetrably mysterious ways, they repeated the idea which had already been expressed off-the-cuff by the cardinal, during the first few hours of the crisis, in the phone conversation he'd had with the prime minister, when, imagining himself to be the pope and asking god to forgive him for such foolish presumption, he had proposed the immediate publication of a new thesis, that of death postponed, trusting in the oft-praised wisdom of time, which tells us that there will always be a tomorrow in which to resolve the problems that today seem insoluble. In a letter to the editor of his favourite newspaper, a reader declared himself perfectly prepared to accept the idea that death had decided to postpone herself, but asked, with the greatest respect, if he could be told how the church had known about this, and that if they really were so well-informed, then they must also know how long the postponement would last. In an editor's note, the newspaper reminded the reader that it was merely a proposal, and one that had not as yet been put into practice, which must mean, he concluded, that the church knew as much about the matter as we did, that is, nothing. At this point, someone wrote an article demanding that the debate return to the question that had started it in the first place, was death one or several, should we be referring to death in the singular or death in the plural, and now that I have my pen in my hand, I would just like to say that the church, in adopting such an ambiguous stance, is merely trying to gain time and avoiding having to commit itself, which is why, as usual, it's busily trying to put a splint on a frog's leg, meanwhile running with the hare and hunting with the hounds. The first of these popular expressions caused some perplexity amongst journalists, who had never heard or read it in their lives before. So, faced by this enigma, and driven on by a healthy dose of professional competitiveness, they hauled down from the shelves the dictionaries they occasionally consulted when writing their articles and news items and set about discovering what that batrachian was doing there. They found nothing, or, rather, they found the frog, they found the leg, they found the splint, but what they didn't manage to do was to get at the meaning those three words clearly had when put together. Then it occurred to one of them to summon an old porter who had arrived from the provinces many years before and whom everyone laughed at because, despite all that time spent living in the city, he still spoke as if he were sitting by the fireside telling stories to his grandchildren. They asked him if he knew the expression and he said, yes, he did, they asked if he knew what it meant and he said, yes, he did. Explain it then, said the editor-in-chief, A splint, gentlemen, is a piece of wood used to hold a broken bone in place, That much we know, but what has it got to do with the frog, It has everything to do with the frog, because no one could ever put a splint on a frog's leg, Why not, Because a frog never keeps its legs still for long enough, So what does the expression mean then, It means that there's no point in trying, because the frog won't let you, But that can't be what the reader meant to say, Well, it's also used when someone is clearly just playing for time, that's when we say they're trying to put a splint on a frog's leg, And that's what the church is doing, Yes, sir, So the reader who wrote this is entirely right, Yes, I believe so, although, of course, my job is keeping an eye on who comes in and out of that door, You've been very helpful, Don't you want me to explain the other expression, Which one, The one about the hare and the hounds, No, we know that one, we practise it every day.

The polemic about death singular or deaths plural, which was started by the spirit hovering over the water in the aquarium and by the apprentice philosopher, would have ended either in comedy or in farce had the article by the economist not appeared. Although, as he himself acknowledged, actuarial calculus was not his speciality, he considered himself sufficiently knowledgeable about the subject to go public and to ask just how, in about twenty years' time, give or take a year, the country thought it would be able to pay the millions of people who would find themselves on permanent disability pensions and would continue like that for all eternity and would, implacably, be joined by further millions, now regardless of whether you used an arithmetic or a geometric progression, disaster was assured, it would mean chaos, disorder, state bankruptcy, a case of sauve qui peut, except that no one would be saved. Confronted by this terrifying vision, the metaphysicians had no option but to button their lip, the church had no option but to return to their weary telling of beads and to waiting for the end of time, which, according to their eschatological visions, would resolve everything once and for all. In fact, going back to the economist's worrying arguments, the calculations were very easy to make, if a certain proportion of the active population are paying their national insurance, and a certain proportion of the inactive population are retired, either for reasons of old age or disability, and therefore drawing on the active population for their pensions, and the active population is constantly on the decrease with respect to the inactive population, and the inactive population is constantly on the increase, it's hard to understand why no one saw at once that the disappearance of death, apparently the peak, the pinnacle, the supreme happiness, was not, after all, a good thing. The philosophers and other abstractionists had first to get lost in the forest of their own lucubrations about the almost and the zero, which is the plebeian way of saying being and nothingness, before common sense could arrive prosaically, with pen and paper in hand, to demonstrate by a + b + c that there were certain far more urgent matters to consider. As was foreseeable, knowing as one does the darker side of human nature, when the economist's alarming article was published, the attitude of the healthy section of the population towards the terminally dying began to change for the worse. Up until then, even though everyone was agreed that the old and the sick caused considerable upsets and problems, it was nevertheless felt that treating them with respect was one of the essential duties of any civilised society, and consequently, although it did occasionally take some effort, the care they needed was never denied to them and, in a few rare cases, this care was even sweetened with a spoonful of compassion and love before the light was turned out. It's also true, as we well know, that there were a few cruel families who allowed themselves to be carried away by their own incurable inhumanity and went so far as to employ the services of the maphia to get rid of the miserable human remains that lay dying interminably between sheets drenched in sweat and stained by natural excretions, but they deserve our disapprobation, as does the family described in the oft-told tale of the wooden bowl, although, fortunately, as you will see, they were saved at the last moment from the final execration thanks to the kind heart of a child of eight. It is a tale quickly told, and we will leave it here for the illumination of new generations who do not know it, in the hope that they do not mock it for being ingenuous or sentimental. Listen, then, to this moral lesson. Once upon a time, in the ancient land of fables, there was a family consisting of a father, a mother, a grandfather who was the father's father, and the aforementioned child of eight, a little boy. Now the grandfather was very old and because of that his hands shook and when he was at table he sometimes dropped his food, to the great irritation of his son and his daughter-in-law, who were always telling him to eat more carefully, but the poor old man, however hard he tried, could not stop his shaking, which only got worse when they told him off, and so he was always staining the tablecloth or dropping food on the floor, not to mention on the napkin they tied around his neck and which they had to change three times a day, at lunch, dinner and supper. This was how things stood, with no hope of improvement, when the son decided to put a stop to the unpleasant situation. He arrived home with a wooden bowl and said to his father, From now on, you'll eat here, sitting on the doorstep, because that's easier to clean, and your daughter-in-law won't have to deal with all those dirty tablecloths and napkins. And so it was. Lunch, dinner and supper, the old man sat alone on the doorstep, raising the food to his mouth as best he could, losing half on the way, while part of the other half dribbled onto his chin, with very little actually making it down what common folk would call his gullet. The grandson seemed entirely unmoved by the cruel treatment being meted out to his grandfather, he would look at him, then look at his mother and father, and continue to eat as if it were none of his business. Then one afternoon, when the father came home from work, he saw his son carving a piece of wood and assumed he was making himself a toy, as was normal in those distant days. The following day, however, he realised that the boy wasn't making a toy car, or at least if he was, he couldn't see where the wheels would go, and so he asked, What are you making. The boy pretended he hadn't heard and continued whittling away at the wood with the point of his knife, this happened in the days when parents were less fearful and wouldn't immediately snatch from their children's hands such a useful tool for making toys. Didn't you hear me, I asked what you're making with that piece of wood, the father asked again, and his son, without glancing up from what he was doing, replied, I'm making a bowl for when you're old and your hands shake and you're sent to sit on the front step to eat your meals, like you did with grandpa. These words had a magical effect. The scales fell from the father's eyes, he saw the truth and its light, and went at once to ask his own father's forgiveness, and when supper-time arrived, he helped him sit down in the chair, fed him with a spoon and gently wiped his chin, because he could still do that, and his dear father could not. History fails to recount what happened afterwards, but we know for certain that the boy's carving was interrupted and the piece of wood is still there. No one wanted to throw it away, perhaps because they didn't want the lesson to be forgotten or because they thought that someone might one day decide to finish the job, which was all too possible when one bears in mind the enormous capacity for survival of the aforesaid darker side of human nature. As someone once said, Everything that can happen will happen, it's only a matter of time, and if we don't get to see it while we're around, it will be because we didn't live long enough. Anyway, just so that we're not accused of painting everything with colours drawn only from the left-hand side of the palette, some believe that an adaptation of this gentle story for television, some newspaper having first rescued it from the dusty shelves of the collective memory and brushed off the cobwebs, might help to restore to the shattered consciences of families the cult or cultivation of the incorporeal values of spirituality once nurtured by society, before the base materialism that currently prevails took possession of wills we imagined to be strong, but which were, in fact, the very image of a dreadful and incurable moral weakness. Let us not, however, give up hope. We are convinced that the moment the boy appears on the screen, half the country's population will race off in search of a handerkchief to dry their tears and the other half, being perhaps of a more stoical temperament, will allow the tears to roll down their face in silence, the better to show that remorse for some evil done or condoned is not necessarily an empty word. Let us hope we are still in time to save the grandparents.

Unexpectedly, and revealing a deplorably poor sense of timing, the republicans decided to choose this delicate occasion to make their voices heard. There were not many of them, they did not even have any representation in parliament, despite forming a political party and regularly standing for election. Nevertheless, they bragged about having a certain amount of social influence, especially in artistic and literary circles, whence came occasional manifestos which while, on the whole, well written, were invariably bland and anodyne. They had shown no sign of life since the disappearance of death, not even, as one might expect from a supposedly radical opposition, in order to demand an explanation for the maphia's rumoured participation in the ignoble traffic in the terminally dying. Now, taking advantage of the anxiety sweeping the country, torn as it was between the vanity of knowing itself to be unique on the whole planet and a feeling of deep disquiet because it was not like anywhere else, there they were bringing into question neither more nor less than the matter of the regime. Being, by definition, opponents of the monarchy and enemies of the throne, they thought they had discovered a new argument in favour of the necessary and urgent establishment of the republic. They said that it went against common logic for a country to have a king who would never die and who, even if he were to decide to abdicate tomorrow for reasons of age or declining mental health, would continue to be king, the first in an endless succession of enthronements and abdications, an endless sequence of kings lying in their beds awaiting a death that would never arrive, a stream of half-alive, half-dead kings who, unless they were kept in the corridors of the palace, would end up filling and finally overflowing the pantheon where their mortal ancestors had been received and who would now be nothing but bones detached from their hinges or musty, mummified remains. How much more logical it would be to have a president of the republic with a fixed term of office, a single mandate, at most two, and then he could go his own sweet way, live his own life, give lectures, write books, take part in congresses, colloquia and symposia, argue his point at round tables, go around the world in eighty receptions, opine upon the length of skirts when they come back into fashion and on the reduction of ozone in the atmosphere if there is an atmosphere, he could, in short, do as he pleased. Better that than having to read every day in the newspapers and hear on television and radio the unalterable medical bulletin, still no change, about the patients in the royal infirmaries, which, it should be noted, having already been extended twice, would be about to be extended again. The plural of infirmaries is there to indicate that, as always happens with hospitals and the like, the men were kept separate from the women, that is, kings and princes on one side, queens and princesses on the other. The republicans were now challenging the people to assume their rightful responsibilities, to take destiny in their hands in order to inaugurate a new life and forge a new, flowerstrewn path towards future dawns. This time their manifesto touched not only artists and writers, other social strata proved equally receptive to the happy image of the flower-strewn path and to those invocations of future dawns, and the result was an absolutely extraordinary flood of support from new militants ready to set off on a crusade which, just as a fish is a fish before and after it has been fished, had passed into history even before anyone knew it would turn out to be an historic event. Unfortunately, in the days that followed, the verbal manifestations of civic enthusiasm from the new supporters of this forward-looking, prophetic republicanism were not always as respectful as good manners and healthy democratic coexistence demand. Some even crossed the line of the most offensive vulgarity, saying, for example, when speaking of their royal highnesses, that they were not prepared to keep donkeys or dumb beasts with rings through their noses supplied with sponge cake. All people of good taste agreed that such words were not just inadmissible, they were unforgivable. It would have sufficed to say that the state's coffers would be unable to continue to support the continual increase in expenditure of the royal household and its adjuncts, and everyone would have understood. It was true, but it did not offend.

It was this violent attack by the republicans, but, more importantly, the article's worrying prediction that, very soon, the aforementioned state coffers would be unable, with no end in sight, to continue paying old age and disability pensions, that prompted the king to let the prime minister know that they needed to have a frank conversation, alone, without tape-recorders or witnesses of any kind. The prime minister duly arrived, enquired after the royal health, in particular after that of the queen mother, who, at new year, had been on the point of dying, but who nonetheless, like so very many others, still continued to breathe thirteen times a minute, even though her prostrate body beneath the canopy covering her bed showed few other signs of life. His majesty thanked him and said that the queen mother was bearing her sufferings with the dignity proper to the blood that still ran in her veins, and then turned to the matters on the agenda, the first of which was the republicans' declaration of war. I just don't understand what these people can be thinking of, he said, here's the country plunged in the worst crisis of its entire history, and there they are talking about regime change, Oh, I wouldn't worry, sir, all they're doing is taking advantage of the situation to spread what they call their plans for government, deep down, they're nothing but poor anglers fishing in some very murky waters, And, let it be said, showing a lamentable lack of patriotism. Indeed, sir, the republicans have ideas about the nation that only they can understand, if, that is, they do understand them, Their ideas don't interest me in the least, what I want to hear from you is if there's any chance they might force a change of regime, They don't even have any representation in parliament, sir, What I'm referring to is a coup d'état, a revolution, Absolutely not, sir, the people are solidly behind their king, and the armed forces are loyal to the legitimate government, So I can rest easy, Completely, sir. The king made a cross in his diary next to the word republicans, and said, Good, then he asked, And what's all this about pensions not being paid, We are paying them, sir, but prospects do look pretty bleak, So I must have misread it, I thought there had been, shall we say, a suspension of payments, No, sir, but, as I say, the future is very worrying indeed, Worrying in what respect, In every respect, sir, the state could simply collapse like a house of cards, Are we the only country that finds itself in this situation, asked the king, No, sir, in the long term, the problem will affect everyone, but what counts is the difference between dying and not dying, a fundamental difference, if you'll forgive me stating the obvious, Sorry, but I don't quite understand, In other countries, it's normal for people to die, but here, sir, in our country, no one dies, think only of the queen mother, it seemed certain she was dying, but, no, she's still here, happily for us, of course, but really, I'm not exaggerating, the noose is well and truly around our necks, And yet I've heard rumours that some people are dying, That's true, sir, but it's merely a drop in the ocean, not all families can bring themselves to take that step, What step, Handing over their dying to the organisation in charge of the suicides, But I don't understand, what's the point of them committing suicide if they can't die, Oh, they can, sir, And how do they manage it, It's a complicated story, sir, Well, tell it to me, we're alone, On the other side of the frontier, sir, people are still dying, You mean that this organisation takes them there, Exactly, Is it a charitable organisation, It helps us a little to slow down the mounting numbers of the terminally dying, but, as I said before, it's a drop in the ocean, And what is this organisation. The prime minister took a deep breath and said, The maphia, sir, The maphia, Yes, sir, the maphia, sometimes the state has no alternative but to find someone else to do its dirty work, You've never said anything to me about this before, No, sir, I wanted to keep you out of a situation for which I take full responsibility, And the troops who were on the frontier, They had a job to do, What job was that, Of appearing to be an obstacle to the transportation of suicides, but not, in fact, being an obstacle at all, But I thought they were there to prevent an invasion, There never was such a danger, and, besides, we've made agreements with the governments of those other countries, and everything's under control, Apart from the matter of pensions, Apart from the matter of death, sir, if we don't start dying again, we have no future. The king made a cross beside the word pensions and said, Something needs to happen, Indeed, sir, something needs to happen.

THE ENVELOPE WAS ON THE DIRECTOR-GENERAL'S DESK WHEN THE secretary went into the office. It was violet-coloured and, therefore, unusual, and the paper had been embossed to resemble the texture of linen. It looked rather antique and gave the impression that it had been used before. There was no address, neither the sender's, which does occasionally happen, nor the addressee's, which never happens, and it was found in an office whose locked door had just been opened, and through which no one could have entered during the night. When she turned the envelope over to see if there was anything written on the back, the secretary felt herself thinking, with a vague sense that it was absurd both to have thought or felt such a thing, that the envelope hadn't been there when she put the key in the lock and turned it. Ridiculous, she murmured, I must simply not have noticed it here when I left yesterday. She glanced round the room to make sure everything was in order and then withdrew to her own desk. In her role as secretary, and a confidential secretary to boot, she had authorisation to open that or any other envelope, especially since it bore no label indicating that it contained restricted information, nothing saying personal, private or secret, and yet she hadn't opened it, and she couldn't understand why. Twice she got up from her chair and opened the door of the office just a crack. The envelope was still there. I'm going crazy, she thought, it must be the colour, I wish he would come now and put an end to the mystery. She was referring to her boss, the director-general of television, who was late. It was a quarter past ten when he finally arrived. Being a man of few words, he merely said good morning and went straight into his office, leaving his secretary with orders to join him in five minutes, the time he considered necessary to settle in and light his first cigarette of the day. When the secretary went into the room, the director-general had not yet taken off his coat or lit a cigarette. He was holding a sheet of paper the same colour as the envelope, and his hands were shaking. He turned to the secretary as she approached the desk, but it was as if he didn't recognise her. He held up one hand to stop her coming nearer and said in a voice that seemed to emerge from someone else's throat, Get out this instant, close that door and don't allow anyone, anyone, you understand, to come in, it doesn't matter who they are. The secretary asked solicitously if anything was wrong, but he interrupted her angrily, Didn't you hear me, he said, I told you to get out. And almost shouting, he added, Get out, now. The poor woman withdrew, with tears in her eyes, she wasn't used to such behaviour, the director has his faults, it's true, like everyone else, but he's generally very polite and not in the habit of treating his secretary like a doormat. It's something to do with that letter, there's no other explanation, she thought while she looked for a handkerchief to dry her eyes. She was quite right. If she dared go back into the office now, she would see the director-general pacing furiously from one side of the room to the other, with a wild expression on his face, as if he didn't know what to do and yet was, at the same time, all too aware that he, and only he, could do it. He looked at his watch, looked at the piece of paper, and murmured very softly, almost to himself, There's still time, there's still time, then he sat down and re-read the mysterious letter, meanwhile mechanically running his other hand over his head, as if to make sure it was still in its place and had not been swallowed up by the vortex of fear gripping his stomach. He stopped reading and sat staring into space, thinking, I must talk to someone, then a thought came to his aid, the idea that it might be a joke, a joke in the worst possible taste, a disgruntled viewer, of whom there are so many, and one with a very macabre imagination indeed, for as anyone high up in the world of television knows, it's definitely no bed of roses, But people don't usually write to me to let off steam, he thought. Needless to say, it was this idea that finally led him to phone through to his secretary and ask, Who brought this letter, I don't know, sir, when I arrived and unlocked the door to your office, just as I always do, there it was, But that's impossible, no one has access to this office at night, Exactly, sir, Then how do you explain it, Don't ask me, sir, I tried to explain what had happened, but you didn't give me a chance, Yes, I'm sorry, I was a little brusque with you, That's all right sir, but it upset me a lot. The director-general again lost patience, If I told you what was in this letter, you'd know the real meaning of being upset. And he hung up. He looked again at his watch, then said to himself, It's the only way out, I can see no other, there are some decisions I can't make. He opened his address book, looked for the number he wanted and found it, Here it is, he said. His hands were still shaking so much that he found it hard to press the right buttons and even harder to control his voice when someone answered, Put me through to the prime minister's office, will you, it's the director-general of television. The cabinet secretary came on the line, Good morning, director-general, it's good to hear you, how can I help, Look, I need to see the prime minister as soon as possible on a matter of extreme urgency, Can't you tell me what it's about so that I can forewarn the prime minister, No, I'm very sorry, but I can't, the matter, as well as urgent, is strictly confidential, But if you could just give me an idea, Listen, I have in my possession a document which has been read only by these eyes that will one day be consumed by the earth, a document of transcendent national importance, and if that's not enough for you to put me straight through to the prime minister wherever he may be, then I very much fear for your personal and political future, So it's serious, All I can say is, from now on, each wasted minute is your sole responsibility, In that case, I'll see what I can do, but the prime minister is very busy, Well, if you want to get yourself a medal, unbusy him, Right away, Fine, I'll hang on, May I ask you another question, Oh, really, what else do you want to know, Why did you use that expression about these eyes that will one day be consumed by the earth, that's what used to happen before, Look, I don't know what you were before, but I know what you are now, a total idiot, now put me through to the prime minister, this instant. The director-general's unexpectedly harsh words show to what extent his mind was disturbed. He's in the grip of a kind of confusion, he doesn't know himself, he can't understand how he could possibly have insulted someone who had merely asked him a question that was perfectly reasonable, both in its terms and its intention. I'll have to apologise, he thought remorsefully, who knows when I might need his help. The prime minister's voice sounded impatient, What's wrong, he asked, as far as I know I don't normally deal with problems to do with television, it's not my business, It's not about television, prime minister, I've received a letter, Yes, they mentioned that you'd had a letter, and what do you want me to do about it, Just read it, that's all, beyond that, to use your own words, it's not my business, You seem upset, Yes, prime minister, I'm extremely upset, And what does this mysterious letter say, I can't tell you over the phone, It's a secure line, No, I still can't tell you, one can't be too careful, Then send it to me, No, I'll have to deliver it myself, I don't want to run the risk of sending a courier, Well, I can send someone from here, my cabinet secretary, for example, he's about as close to me as anyone, Prime minister, please, I wouldn't be bothering you if I didn't have a very good reason, I really must see you, When, Now, But I'm busy, Prime minister, please, All right, if you insist, come and see me, and I just hope all this mystery is worth it, Thank you, I'll be right there. The director-general put down the phone, replaced the letter in its envelope, slipped it into one of the inside pockets in his overcoat and got up. His hands had stopped shaking, but his face was dripping sweat. He wiped the sweat away with his handkerchief, then spoke to his secretary on the internal phone, told her he was going out and asked her to call the car. The fact of having passed responsibility to another person calmed him a little, in half an hour his role in the matter will be over. The secretary appeared at the door, The car's waiting, sir, Thank you, I'm not sure how long I'll be, I have a meeting with the prime minister, but that information is for you alone, Don't worry, sir, I won't tell anyone, Goodbye, Goodbye, sir, I hope everything turns out for the best, In the current state of affairs, we no longer know what's for the best and what's for the worst, You're right, By the way, how's your father, Just the same, sir, he doesn't actually seem to be suffering, he's simply wasting away, burning out, he's been like that for the last two months, and given how things are going, it's just a matter of waiting my turn to lie down in a bed next to his, Who knows, said the director-general, and left.

The cabinet secretary received the director-general at the door and greeted him with evident coldness, then he said, I'll take you to the prime minister, One moment, first I want to apologise, if there was a total idiot in our conversation, it was me, It probably wasn't either of us, said the cabinet secretary, smiling, If you could read what I have in my pocket, you would understand my state of mind, Don't worry, as far as I'm concerned, you're forgiven, Thank you, it won't be long now before the bomb explodes and then everyone will know about it, Let's hope it doesn't make too much noise when it goes off, The noise will be louder than the loudest thunder ever heard, and the lightning brighter than all the lightning ever seen, You're starting to frighten me, At that point, my friend, I'm sure you'll forgive me again, Come on, the prime minister's waiting. They crossed a room, one that, in ages past, would have been called an anteroom, and a minute later, the director-general was in the presence of the prime minister, who received him with a smile, So what's this life-or-death problem you've brought me, With all due respect, prime minister, I doubt you've ever spoken more aptly. He took the letter from his pocket and held it out to him across the table. The prime minister was puzzled, It doesn't have an addressee, Nor the name of the person who sent it, said the director-general, it's as if it were a letter addressed to everyone, Anonymous, No, prime minister, as you'll see, it is signed, but read it, read it, please. The envelope was slowly opened, the piece of paper unfolded, but after reading only the first few lines, the prime minister looked up and said, This must be a joke, It could be, yes, but I don't think so, it appeared on my desk and no one knows how, That doesn't seem a very good reason why we should believe what it says, Read on, please. When he reached the end of the letter, the prime minister, very slowly, silently moving his lips, articulated the one syllable of the word that served as signature. He put the letter down on the desk, stared across at the director-general and said, Let's imagine it's just a joke, It isn't, No, I'm inclined to believe it isn't either, but when I say let's imagine, it's only to conclude that it won't be many hours before we find out, Precisely twelve hours, given that it's midday now, That's my point, if what the letter tells us is going to happen does actually come to pass, and if we don't warn people, there'll be a repetition, only in reverse, of what happened on new year's eve, It doesn't make any difference whether we warn them or not, prime minister, the effect will be the same, But opposite, Yes, opposite, but the same, Exactly, so if we warned them and it turned out afterwards that it was all a joke, we'd have worried people unnecessarily, although there would be much to say about the pertinence of that adverb, No, I really don't think it's worth it, and you've already said you don't think it's a joke, No, I don't, So what's to be done, to warn or not to warn, That is the question, my dear director-general, we must think, ponder, reflect, The matter is now in your hands, prime minister, the decision is yours, It is indeed, I could even tear this piece of paper into a thousand pieces and just wait and see what happens, But I don't think you'll do that, You're right, I won't, but a decision must be taken, saying that the population should be warned isn't enough, we have to consider how, That's what the media are for, prime minister, we have the television, the newspapers, the radio, Your idea, then, is that we distribute to all these different media a photocopy of the letter accompanied by a communiqué from the government calling for calm and giving some advice on how to proceed during the emergency, You put it far better than I ever could, Thank you for the compliment, but now I must ask you to try and imagine what would happen if we did exactly that, Um, I don't understand, prime minister, Oh, I expected better from the director-general of television, Then I'm sorry not to be able to rise to the occasion, prime minister, It's only natural, you're overwhelmed by the responsibility, And you are not, prime minister, Yes, I am too, but in my case, overwhelmed doesn't mean paralysed, Fortunately for the country, Thank you again, we've never really talked very much before, well, generally speaking, when I discuss television, I do so with the relevant minister, but I feel the moment has come to make you a national figure, Now I really don't understand, prime minister, It's quite simple, the matter is going to remain strictly between you and me until nine o'clock this evening, at

85

that time, the television news will open with a reading of the official communiqué which will explain what will happen at midnight tonight, as well as a summary of the letter, and the person to be charged with doing both those things is the director-general of television, firstly, because the letter was sent to him, even though it doesn't name him, and secondly, because you, the director-general of television, are the person I trust to get us both through the mission with which, implicitly, we have been charged by the lady who signed this letter, A newsreader would do a better job, prime minister, No, I don't want a newsreader, I want the director-general of television, If that's what you want, then I would consider it an honour, We are the only people who know what is going to happen at midnight tonight and we will continue to be so until the time when the population receives the information, if we were to do what you proposed earlier, that is, pass the news to the media now, we would have twelve hours of confusion, panic, tumult, mass hysteria and who knows what, therefore, since it is not in our power, and I refer here to the government, to avoid such reactions, at least we can limit it to three hours, and from then on it will be beyond our control, there will be all kinds of responses, tears, despair, ill-disguised relief, a need to rethink life, It seems a good idea, Yes, but only because we don't have a better one. The prime minister picked up the letter again, glanced over it without reading it and said, It's odd, the initial letter of the signature should be a capital, but it's not, Yes, I found that odd too, starting a name with a lower case letter isn't normal, Can you see anything normal in this whole affair, Not really, no, By the way, do you know how to make a photocopy, Well, I'm not an expert, but I've done it a few times, Excellent. The prime minister put the letter and the envelope in a file stuffed with documents and summoned the cabinet secretary, to whom he said, Please evacuate the room where the photocopier is, That's where the civil servants work, prime minister, that's their office, Well, tell them to go somewhere else, tell them to wait in the corridor or go out and smoke a cigarette, we'll only need it for three minutes, isn't that right, director-general, Not even that long, prime minister, Look, I can make a photocopy in absolute secrecy, if, as I assume, that is what you want, said the cabinet secretary, That's precisely what we want, secrecy, but, this time, I myself will do the job, with the technical assistance, shall we say, of the director-general, Of course, prime minister, I'll give the necessary orders for the room to be cleared. He came back within minutes, It's empty, prime minister, and now, if I may, I'll go back to my office, And I'm very glad that I don't have to ask you to do so, and please don't be offended by our excluding you from these apparently conspiratorial manoeuvres, you'll find out later today the reason for such precautions and you won't need me to tell you either, Of course, prime minister, I would never doubt the wisdom of your motives, That's the spirit, my friend. When the cabinet secretary left, the prime minister picked up the file and said, Right, let's go. The room was deserted. In less than a minute, the photocopy was ready, letter for letter, word for word, but it was different, it lacked the disquieting touch of the violet-coloured paper, now it's just an ordinary missive, the kind that begin, I do hope these lines find you well and happy and surrounded by your family, as for me, I certainly can't complain. The prime minister handed the copy to the director-general, There you are, I'll keep the original, he said, And the government communiqué, when will I receive that, Sit down and I'll dictate it to you, it won't take a moment, it's very simple, dear compatriots, the government considers that it has a duty to inform the country of a letter that has reached its hands only today, a document whose significance and importance cannot be exaggerated, even though we are not in a position to guarantee its authenticity and must admit, without wishing to anticipate its contents, that there is a possibility that what is announced in the document may not come to pass, however, in order that the population should be mentally prepared for a situation that will not be without its tensions and crises, the letter will now be read out, with the government's approval, by the director-general of television, just one word more before we conclude, the government, needless to say, will, as always, remain alert to the interests and needs of the population during hours which will doubtless be amongst the most difficult we have experienced since we have been a people and a nation, and it is for this reason that we call on you all to preserve the calmness and serenity you have shown so often before during the various trials and tests to which we've been subjected since the beginning of the year, and, at the same time, we trust that a more benevolent future will restore to us the peace and happiness we deserve and which we once enjoyed, remember, dear compatriots, united we stand, that is our motto, our watchword, if we remain united, then the future is ours, there you are, quick work as you see, these official communiqués don't demand any great imaginative effort, they almost write themselves you might say, there's a typewriter over there, make a fair copy and keep it safe until nine o'clock tonight, don't let those papers out of your sight even for a moment, Don't worry, prime minister, I'm keenly aware of my responsibilities at this moment, I'm sure you won't be disappointed, Excellent, now you can go back to work, May I just ask two questions before I leave, Please do, You said that until nine o'clock tonight only two people will know about this matter, Yes, yourself and me, no one else, not even the government, What about the king, and forgive me if I'm butting in where I'm not wanted, His majesty will find out when everyone else finds out, that is, of course, if he happens to be watching television, He won't, I imagine, be very happy not to have been told before, Don't worry, the one excellent quality that all kings share, and I refer, of course, to constitutional monarchs, is that they are extraordinarily understanding, Ah, And your other question, It's not exactly a question, What is it then, Just that I am, quite frankly, astonished at your sangfroid, prime minister, it seems to me that what's going to happen in this country at midnight is a catastrophe, a cataclysm like no other, a kind of end-of-the-world, but when I look at you, it's as if you were merely dealing with some routine government matter, you calmly give your orders, and a little while ago, I even had the impression that you smiled, If you knew how many problems this letter will resolve for me without my having to lift a finger, I'm sure that you would smile too, director-general, now leave me to my work, I have a few orders to issue, I must tell the interior minister to put the police on high alert, I'll think up some plausible excuse, the possibility of some act of public disorder, he's not a person to waste much time on reflection, he prefers action, give him something to do and he's a happy man, Prime minister, may I just say that it's been a real privilege to have lived through this crucial time with you, Well, I'm glad you see it like that, but you can be quite sure that you would quickly change your mind if one word of what has been said in this office, by me or by you, were ever to reach the ears of someone beyond these four walls, Yes, I understand, The ears of a constitutional monarch, for example, Yes, prime minister.

It was almost eight thirty when the director-general summoned to his office the man in charge of the television news to tell him that the programme that night would open with a message from the government to the country as a whole, and would be read, as usual, by the newsreader on duty, after which he himself, the director-general, would read another document to complement the first. If the producer found this procedure odd, unusual, out of the normal run of things, he did not show it, he merely asked to have the two documents so that they could be placed on the autocue, that wonderful piece of apparatus which creates the vain illusion that the person speaking is doing so directly and solely to each member of the audience. The director-general replied that, in this case, the autocue would not be used, We'll simply read it out, as people used to do, he said, adding that he would enter the studio at five to nine precisely, when he would hand the government communiqué to the newsreader, who would be given rigorous instructions that he must only open the file containing it when he was about to begin the reading. The producer thought that now there really was some reason to show a little interest in the matter, Is it that important, he asked, You'll find out in half an hour, And the flag, sir, do you want the flag to be placed behind the chair where you'll be sitting, No, no flags, after all, I'm not the prime minister or even a minister, Nor the king, said the producer, with an ingratiating smile, as if to say that he was the king, the king of television. The director-general ignored him, You can go now, I'll be in the studio in twenty minutes, There won't be time for make-up, I don't want any make-up, what I have to read is very short, and the viewers, at that point, will have more things on their mind than whether or not I'm wearing make-up, Very well, sir, as you wish, But be sure that the lights don't cast too many shadows on my face, I wouldn't want to appear on screen looking like someone who's just been dug up from his grave, especially not tonight. At five to nine, the director-general went into the studio, handed the newsreader the file containing the government communiqué and went and sat in his appointed chair. Attracted by the unprecedented nature of the situation, for the news, as one would expect, had spread fast, there were more people than usual in the studio. The producer called for silence. At nine o'clock exactly, to the accompaniment of the familiar theme tune, the urgent opening titles to the news programme were flashed up, a fast-moving sequence of sundry images intended to convince the viewer that the television station, at their service twenty-four hours a day, was, as used to be said of the divinity, everywhere, and from everywhere sent news. The moment that the newsreader finished reading the government communiqué, camera two brought the director-general up on screen. He was clearly nervous, his mouth dry. He briefly cleared his throat and began to read, dear sir, I wish to inform you and all those concerned that as from midnight tonight people will start to die again, as had always happened, with little protest, from the beginning of time until the thirty-first day of december last year, I should explain that the reason that led me to interrupt my activities, to stop killing and put away the emblematic scythe that imaginative painters and engravers of yore always placed in my hand, was to give those human beings who so loathe me just a taste of what it would mean to live for ever, eternally, although, between you and me, sir, I must confess that I have no idea whether those two expressions, for ever and eternally, are as synonymous as is generally believed, anyway, after this period of a few months of what we might call an endurance test or merely extra time and bearing in mind the deplorable results of the experiment, both from the moral, that is, philosophical point of view, and from the pragmatic, that is, social point of view, I felt that it would be best for families and for society as a whole, both vertically and horizontally, if I acknowledged my mistake publicly and announced an immediate return to normality, which will mean that all those people who should be dead, but who, with health or without it, nevertheless remain in the world, will have the candle of their life snuffed out as the last stroke of midnight fades on the air, and please note that the reference to the last stroke is merely symbolic, just in case someone gets the stupid idea of stopping the clocks in all the belltowers or of removing the clappers from the bells themselves, imagining that this will stop time and contradict my irrevocable decision, that of restoring the supreme fear to the hearts of men   most of the people in the studio had by now disappeared, and those who remained were whispering to each other, the buzz of their murmurings failing to provoke the producer, who was himself standing slack-jawed with amazement, into silencing them with the furious gesture he normally deployed, albeit in far less dramatic circumstances   therefore, resign yourselves and die without protest because it will get you nowhere, however, there is one point on which I feel it my duty to admit that I was wrong, and that has to do with the cruel and unjust way in which I used to proceed, taking people's lives by stealth, with no prior warning, without so much as a by-your-leave, and I recognise that this was downright brutal, often I didn't even allow them time to draw up a will, although it's true that in most cases I did send them an illness to pave the way, but the strange thing about illnesses is that human beings always hope to shake them off, and so only when it's too late do they realise that it will be their final illness, anyway, from now on everyone will receive due warning and be given a week to put what remains of their life in order, to make a will and say goodbye to their family, asking forgiveness for any wrongs done and making peace with the cousin they haven't spoken to for twenty years, and that said, director-general, all I would ask is that you make sure that, today without fail, every home in the land receives this message, which I sign with the name I am usually known by, death. When he saw that his image had gone from the screen, the director-general got up from his chair, folded the letter and put it in one of his inside jacket pockets. He saw the producer coming towards him, looking pale and distraught, So that's what it was, he said in a barely audible murmur, so that's what it was. The director-general nodded silently and headed for the exit. He didn't hear the words that the newsreader had stammeringly begun to announce, You have just been listening, followed by an account of the other news that had ceased to be of any importance because no one in the country was paying the least attention, in those households where someone lay terminally ill, the families went and gathered round the deathbed, and yet they couldn't tell the dying person that in three hours he would be dead, they couldn't tell him that he should make use of what time remained to write the will he had always refused to write or ask if he wanted to phone his cousin and make his peace with him, nor could they follow the hypocritical custom of asking if he was feeling any better, they simply stood staring at the pale, emaciated face, then glanced surreptitiously at the clock, waiting for the time to pass and for the train of the world to get back on track and make its usual journey. And a number of families who, having already paid the maphia to take away that sad remnant, and imagining that they would probably shed no tears over the money spent, saw now that if they'd had a little more charity and patience, they could have got rid of him for free. There were terrible scenes in the streets, people stood stock-still, stunned or disoriented, not knowing where to run, some wept inconsolably, others embraced as if they'd decided to begin their farewells right there, still others discussed whether the blame for all of this lay with the government or with medical science or with the pope in rome, one sceptic protested that there was no previous record of death ever having written a letter and that it should be sent at once to a handwriting analyst, because, he said, a hand made only of bits of bone would never be able to write like a complete, authentic, living hand, with its blood, veins, nerves, tendons, skin and flesh, and since bones obviously wouldn't leave any fingerprints on the paper, which meant that they wouldn't be able to identify the author of the letter that way, a dna test might throw some light on this unexpected epistolary appearance from a being, if death is a being, who had, until then, remained silent all her life. At this moment, the prime minister is talking on the phone to the king, explaining why he had decided not to tell him about the letter, and the king says that yes, he understands perfectly, then the prime minister tells him how sorry he is about the sad conclusion that the last stroke of midnight will bring to the frail existence of the queen mother, and the king shrugs, such a life is no life at all, today it will be her, tomorrow me, especially now that the heir to the throne is showing signs of impatience and asking when it will be his turn to be constitutional monarch. After this intimate conversation, with its unusual moments of sincerity, the prime minister gave instructions to the cabinet secretary to call all the members of the government together for an emergency meeting, I want them here in forty-five minutes, at ten on the dot, he said, we will have to discuss, approve and put in place the necessary palliative measures to minimise the likely confusion and disorder that the new situation will inevitably provoke in the next few days, Are you referring to the number of dead people who will have to be evacuated in that very short space of time, prime minister, That remains the least of our problems, my friend, the reason funeral directors exist is in order to resolve problems of that nature, besides, the crisis is over for them, and they must be extremely happy as they tot up how much money they're going to earn, so let them bury the dead because that's their job, what we have to do is deal with the living, for example, organise teams of psychiatrists to help people recover from the trauma of having to die when they were convinced they were going to live for ever, Yes, I've thought about that myself, and it will be hard, Don't waste any more time, tell the ministers to bring their respective secretaries of state with them, I want them here at ten o'clock prompt, and if anyone asks, tell them all that they're the first to be called, they're like little children who want their sweeties. The phone rang, it was the interior minister, Prime minister, I'm getting calls from all the newspapers, he said, they demand to be shown the letter that has just been read out on television in the name of death, and about which, regrettably, I knew nothing, There's no need for regrets, I made the decision to keep it secret so that we wouldn't have to put up with twelve hours of panic and confusion, What shall I do then, Don't worry about it, my office is going to distribute the letter to all the media now, Excellent, prime minister, The cabinet will meet at ten o'clock prompt, bring your secretaries of state, And the under-secretaries too, No, leave them to look after the house, I've often heard it said that too many cooks spoil the broth, Yes, prime minister, Be on time, the meeting will start at one minute past ten, We'll be the first to arrive, prime minister, You'll be sure to get your medal then, What medal is that, It was just a joke, take no notice.

At the same time, the undertakers' representatives, burials, cremations, funerals, round-the-clock service, are going to meet at the same time at the corporation headquarters. Faced by the overwhelming and never before experienced professional challenge that the simultaneous death and subsequent funerary despatch of thousands of people throughout the country will bring with it, the only real solution they can come up with, which also promises to be highly profitable thanks to a rationalised reduction in costs, will be to pool, in a coordinated and orderly fashion, all the personnel and the technological means, in other words, the logistics, at their disposal, establishing along the way proportional quotas for shares in the cake, as the president of the corporation so drolly put it, provoking discreet but amused applause from the other members. They will have to bear in mind, for example, that the production of coffins, tombs, caskets, biers and catafalques for human use had ground to a halt the day people stopped dying and that, in the unlikely event of there being any stock left in some conservatively minded carpenter's shop, it will be like malherbe's little rosebud, which, once transformed into a rose, can last no longer than a morning. This literary reference came from the president who went on to say, rather spoiling the mood, but nevertheless provoking applause from the audience, At least we'll no longer have to suffer the humiliation of having to bury dogs, cats and pet canaries, And parrots, said a voice from the back, Indeed, and parrots, agreed the president, And tropical fish, added another voice, That was only after the controversy caused by the spirit hovering over the water in the aquarium, said the minutes secretary, from now on they'll be thrown to the cats, for as lavoisier said, in nature, nothing is created and nothing is lost, everything is transformed. We never found out quite to what extremes the undertakers' show of almanac wisdom would go because one of their representatives, concerned about the time, a quarter to midnight by his watch, put up his hand to propose telephoning the association of carpenters to ask how many coffins they had, We need to know what supplies we can rely on from tomorrow onwards, he concluded. As one might expect, this proposal was warmly applauded, but the president, barely disguising his pique because he himself had not come up with the idea, remarked, There probably won't be anyone there at this hour, Allow me to disagree, president, the same reasons that brought us together must have prompted them to the same thing. The proposer was absolutely right. The corporation of carpenters replied that they had alerted their respective members as soon as they'd heard the letter from death read out, alerting them to the need to start manufacturing coffins again as soon as possible, and, according to the information coming in all the time, not only had many businesses immediately called in their workers, most were already hard at work. That does, of course, contravene legislation regarding working hours, said the corporation's spokesperson, but, given that we're in a state of national emergency, our lawyers are sure that the government will have no option but to close their eyes to this and will, moreover, be grateful to us, what we cannot guarantee, in this first phase, is that the coffins being supplied will be of the same high quality and finish to which our clients have become accustomed, the polish, the varnishes and the crucifixes on the lid will have to be left for the second phase, when the pressure of funerals starts to diminish, but we are, nevertheless, conscious of the responsibility of being a fundamental part of this process. There was more and still warmer applause amongst that gathering of undertakers' representatives, for now there really were reasons for mutual congratulation, no corpse would be left unburied, no invoice would be left unpaid. And what about the gravediggers, asked the man who had made the proposal, The gravediggers will do as they're told, replied the president irritably. This wasn't quite true. Another phone call revealed that the gravediggers were demanding a substantial salary increase and triple the going rate for any overtime. That's a problem for the local councils, said the president, let them sort it out. And what if we arrive at the cemetery and there's no one to dig the graves, asked the secretary. The debate raged on. At twenty-three hours and fifty minutes, the president had a heart attack. He died on the last stroke of midnight.

IT WAS MUCH MORE THAN A HECATOMB. THE SEVEN MONTHS that death's unilateral truce had lasted produced a waiting list of more than sixty thousand people on the point of death, or sixty-two thousand five hundred and eighty to be exact, all laid to rest in a moment, in an instant of time packed with a deadly power that would find comparison only in certain reprehensible human actions. By the way, we feel we must mention that death, by herself and alone, with no external help, has always killed far less than mankind has. Some curious-minded soul might be wondering how we came up with that precise figure of sixty-two thousand five hundred and eighty people who all closed their eyes at the same time and for ever. It was very easy. Knowing that the country in which this is happening has more or less ten million inhabitants and that the death rate is more or less ten per thousand, two simple, not to say elementary arithmetical operations, multiplication and division, and factoring in, of course, the intermediate monthly and annual rates, allowed us to arrive at a narrow numerical band in which the quantity seemed like a reasonable average, and we use the word reasonable because we could have opted for the numbers on either side, sixty-two thousand five hundred and seventy-nine or sixty-two thousand five hundred and eighty-one if the death of the president of the undertakers' corporation, so sudden and unexpected, had not introduced into our calculations an element of doubt. Nevertheless, we are confident that the count made of the number of deaths, begun first thing the next morning, will confirm the accuracy of our calculations. Another curious-minded soul, of the kind who is always interrupting the narrator, will be wondering how the doctors knew which houses to go to in order to carry out a duty without which no dead person can be deemed legally dead, however indisputably dead they may be. Needless to say, in certain cases, the deceased's own family called out a locum or their GP, but that would clearly not have been enough, since the aim was to try, in record time, to make official an entirely anomalous situation, and thus avoid confirming yet again the saying that misfortunes never come singly, which, when applied to this situation, would mean that any sudden death at home would be swiftly followed by putrefaction. Events went on to show that it is not by chance that a prime minister reaches such lofty heights and that, as the infallible wisdom of nations has demonstrated time and again, each country gets the government it deserves, although it must be said that while it is true to say that prime ministers, for good or ill, are not all the same, nor, it is no less true to say, are all countries. In short, in either case, it depends. Or if you prefer a slightly longer version of the same phrase, you never can tell. As you will see, any observer, even one not prone to making impartial judgements, will not hesitate to acknowledge that the government proved itself able to cope with the gravity of the situation. We will all remember that in the joy to which these people innocently surrendered themselves during those first, delicious and all-too-brief days of immortality, one lady, a recent widow, celebrated this new-found happiness by hanging the national flag from the flower-bedecked balcony of her dining room. We will also recall that, in less than forty-eight hours, this custom spread through the country like wildfire, like an epidemic. After seven months of continual and hard-to-bear disappointments, very few of those flags had survived, and even those that had were reduced to melancholy rags, their colours faded by the sun and washed away by the rains, the central emblem now nothing but a sad blur. Showing admirable foresight, the government, as well as taking other emergency measures intended to mitigate any collateral damage caused by death's unexpected return, had reclaimed for themselves the national flag as a sign that there, on that third-floor apartment on the left, a dead person lay waiting. With these instructions, those families wounded by the odious parcae sent one of their members to the shop to buy a new flag, hung it at the window, and, as they brushed the flies from the face of the deceased, waited for the doctor to come and certify the death. It must be acknowledged that the idea was not just effective, but also extremely elegant. The doctors in each city, town, village or hamlet, in a car, on a bicycle or on foot, had only to wander the streets looking for a flag, go into the house thus marked and, having confirmed the death after a purely visual examin-ation, without the help of instruments, since the scale of the emergency had made any closer scrutiny unfeasible, leave a signed piece of paper that would reassure the undertakers as to the specific nature of the raw material, which is to say, that, as the proverb goes, if they came to this house of the dead looking for wool, they would not go home shorn. As you will have realised, this clever use of the national flag would have a double aim and a double advantage. Having started out as a guide for doctors, it would then be a beacon for those who came to prepare the body. In the case of larger cities, and espe-cially in the capital, which was a vast metropolis given the rela-tively small size of the country, the division of urban areas into sections, with a view to establishing proportional quotas for shares in the cake, as the unfortunate president of the associ-ation of funeral directors had so pithily put it, would prove an enormous help to the transporters of human freight in their race against time. The flag had another unforeseen and unexpected effect, one that shows how wrong we can be when we systematically devote ourselves to the cultivation of scepticism, and this was the virtuous gesture performed by certain citizens who were both respecters of the most deeply rooted traditions of polite social conduct as well as wearers of hats, for they would doff said hats whenever they passed a window adorned with a flag, thus leaving floating in the air a delightful doubt as to whether they were doing so because someone had died or because the flag was the living, sacred symbol of the nation.

Sales of newspapers, we hardly need say, shot up, even more so than when it seemed that death was a thing of the past. Obviously a lot of people had already heard on television about the cataclysm that had befallen them, many even had dead relatives at home awaiting the doctor's arrival, along with a flag weeping on the balcony outside, but it's easy to understand that there is a difference between the nervous image of the director-general talking last night on the small screen and these convulsive, agitated pages, emblazoned with exclamatory, apocalyptic headlines that can be folded up and put in one's pocket and carried off to be re-read at leisure in one's home and of which we are pleased to present a few of the more striking examples here, After Paradise, Hell, Death Leads The Dance, Immortal But Not For Long, Once More Condemned To Die, Checkmate, Prior Warning From Now On, No Appeal And No Hope, A Letter On Violet Paper, Sixty-Two Thousand Deaths In Less Than A Second, Death Strikes At Midnight, No Escape From Destiny, Out Of the Dream And Into the Nightmare, Return To Normal, What Did We Do To Deserve This, etcetera, etcetera. All the newspapers, without exception, reprinted death's letter on the front page, but one of them, to make it easier to read, reproduced the text in a box and in a fourteen-point font, corrected the punctuation and syntax, adjusted the tenses of the verbs, added capitals where necessary, including on the final signature, which was changed from death to Death, an alteration unappreciable by the ear, but which, that same day, would provoke an indignant protest from the writer of the missive herself, again using the same violet-coloured paper. According to the authorised opinion of a grammarian consulted by the newspaper, death had simply failed to master even the first rudiments of the art of writing. And then, he said, there's the calligraphy, which is strangely irregular, it's as if it combined all the known ways, both possible and aberrant, of forming the letters of the latin alphabet, as if each had been written by a different person, but that could be forgiven, one could even consider it a minor defect given the chaotic syntax, the absence of full stops, the complete lack of very necessary parentheses, the obsessive elimination of paragraphs, the random use of commas and, most unforgivable sin of all, the intentional and almost diabolical abolition of the capital letter, which, can you imagine, is even omitted from the actual signature of the letter and replaced by a lower-case d. It was a disgrace, an insult, the grammarian went on, asking, If death, who has had the priceless privilege of seeing the great literary geniuses of the past, writes like this, what of our children if they choose to imitate such a philological monstrosity, on the excuse that, considering how long death has been around, she should know everything there is to know about all branches of knowledge. And the grammarian concluded, The syntactical blunders that fill this appalling letter would lead me to think that this was some huge, clumsy confidence trick were it not for grim reality and the painful evidence that the terrible threat has come to pass. As we mentioned, on the afternoon of that same day, a letter from death reached the newspaper, demanding, in the most energetic terms, that the original spelling of her name be restored, Dear sir, she wrote, I am not Death, but death, Death is something of which you could never even conceive, and please note, mister grammarian, that I did not conclude that phrase with a preposition, you human beings only know the small everyday death that is me, the death which, even in the very worst disasters, is incapable of preventing life from continuing, one day you will find out about Death with a capital D, and at that moment, in the unlikely event that she gives you time to do so, you will understand the real difference between the relative and the absolute, between full and empty, between still alive and no longer alive, and when I say real difference, I am referring to something that mere words will never be able to express, relative, absolute, full, empty, still alive and no longer alive, because, sir, in case you don't know it, words move, they change from one day to the next, they are as unstable as shadows, are themselves shadows, which both are and have ceased to be, soap bubbles, shells in which one can barely hear a whisper, mere tree stumps, I give you this information gratis and for free, meanwhile, concern yourself with explaining to your readers the whys and wherefores of life and death, and now, returning to the original purpose of this letter, written, as was the one read out on television, by my own hand, I ask you to fulfill the provisions contained in the press regulations which demand that any error, omission or mistake be rectified on the same page and in the same font-size, and if this letter is not published in full, sir, you run the risk of receiving tomorrow morning, with immediate effect, the prior warning that I was reserving for you in a few years' time, although, so as not to ruin the rest of your life, I won't say exactly how many, yours faithfully, death. Accompanied by fulsome apologies from the editor, the letter appeared punctually the next day and in duplicate too, that is, reproduced in manuscript form as well as boxed and in the same fourteen-point font. Only when the newspaper was distributed did the editor dare to emerge from the bunker in which he had been hidden away from the moment he had read that threatening letter. And he was so frightened that he even refused to publish the graphological study delivered to him personally by an important expert. I got myself in quite enough of a mess just by printing death's signature with an upper case d, so take your analysis to some other newspaper, let's share out the misfortune and from now on leave things to god, anything to avoid getting another fright like that. The graphologist went to another newspaper, then another and another, and only at the fourth try, when he was already losing hope, did he find someone prepared to accept the fruits of the many hours of labyrinthine work he had put in, toiling day and night over his magnifying glass. The substantial and juicy report began by noting that the interpretation of writing had originally been one of the branches of physiognomy, the others being, for the information of those not au fait with this exact science, mime, gesture, pantomime and phonognomy, after which he brought in the major authorities on this complex subject, each in his or her own time and place, for example, camillo baldi, johann caspar lavater, édouard auguste patrice hocquart, adolf henze, jean-hippolyte michon, william thierry preyer, cesare lombroso, jules crépieux-jamin, rudolf pophal, ludwig klages, wilhelm helmuth müller, alice enskat, robert heiss, thanks to whom graphology had been restructured as a psychological tool, demonstrating the ambivalence of graphological details and the need to express these as a whole, and then, having set out the essential historical facts of the matter, our graphologist launched into an exhaustive definition of the principal characteristics being studied, namely, size, pressure, spacing, margins, angles, punctuation, the length of upward and downward strokes, or, in other words, the intensity, shape, slant, direction and fluidity of graphic signs, and finally, having made it clear that the aim of his study was not to make a clinical diagnosis, or a character analysis, or an examination of professional aptitude, the specialist focussed his attention on the evident links with the criminological world which the writing revealed at every step, Nevertheless, he wrote in grim, frustrated tones, I find myself faced by a contradiction which I can see no way of resolving, and for which I very much doubt there is any possible resolution, and this is the fact that while it is true that all the vectors of this methodical and meticulous graphological analysis point to the authoress of the letter being what people call a serial killer, another equally irrefutable truth finally imposed itself upon me, one that to some extent demolishes that earlier thesis, which is this, that the person who wrote the letter is dead. And so it was, and death herself could not but confirm this, You're quite right, sir, she said when she read this display of erudition. What no one could understand was this, if she was dead and nothing but bones, how then could she kill? More to the point, how could she write letters? These are mysteries that will never be explained.

Occupied as we were with explaining what happened after the fateful stroke of midnight to the sixty-two thousand five hundred and eighty people left in a state of suspended life, we put off for a more opportune moment, which happens to be this one, our indispensable reflections on the way in which the changed situation affected the eventide homes, the hospitals, the insurance companies, the maphia and the church, especially the catholic church, which was the country's majority religion, so much so that it was commonly believed that our lord jesus christ would not have wanted to be born anywhere else if he had had to repeat, from a to z, his first and, as far as we know, only earthly existence. To begin with the eventide homes, feelings were much as you would expect. If you bear in mind, as we explained at the very start of these surprising events, that the continuous rotation of inmates was a necessary condition for the economic prosperity of these enterprises, the return of death was bound to be, and indeed was, a reason for joy and renewed hope for the respective managements. After the initial shock provoked by the reading out on television of the famous letter from death, the managers immediately began to do their sums and they all came out right. Not a few bottles of champagne were drunk at midnight to celebrate this unexpected return to normality, and while such behaviour may appear to show a gross indifference to and scorn for other people's lives, what it really showed was the perfectly natural sense of relief, the need to give vent to pent-up emotions, of someone who, standing outside a locked door to which he has lost the key, suddenly sees it swing open and the sun come pouring in. More scrupulous people will say that they should at least have avoided the noisy, frivolous ostentation of champagne, with corks popping and glasses overflowing, and that a discreet glass of port or madeira, a drop of cognac, a touch of brandy in one's coffee would have been celebration enough, but we know how easily the spirit lets slip the reins of the body when happiness takes over, and know, too, that even though one shouldn't condone it, one can always forgive. The following morning, the managers summoned the families to fetch their dead, then they had the rooms aired and the sheets changed, and, having gathered all the staff together to tell them that life goes on despite all, they sat down to examine the list of potential customers and to choose from amongst the applicants those who seemed most promising. For reasons not entirely identical in every aspect, but which, nevertheless, merit equal consideration, the mood amongst hospital administrators and the medical classes had also improved overnight. However, as we said before, although a large number of patients who were beyond cure or whose illness had reached its end or its final stage, if one can apply such terms to a nosological state deemed to be eternal, had been moved back to their homes and their families, What better hands could the poor wretches find themselves in, they asked hypocritically, the truth is that many of them, with no known relatives and no money to pay the rates demanded by the eventide homes, were crammed in wherever there was space, not in corridors, as has long been the custom in these worthy establishments yesterday, today and always, but in lumber rooms and attics, where they would often be left for days at a time, without anyone taking the slightest notice of them, for, as the doctors and nurses said, regardless of how ill they might be, they couldn't die. Now they were dead, and had been taken away and buried, and the air in the hospitals, with its unmistakable aroma of ether, iodine and disinfectant, had become as pure and crystalline as mountain air. They didn't crack open any bottles of champagne, but the happy smiles of administrators and clinical directors were a salve to the soul, and as for the male doctors, suffice it to say that they had recovered their traditionally predatory gaze when they gave the female nursing staff the eye. Normality, in every sense of the word, had been restored. As for the insurance companies, third on the list, there is not as yet much to say, because they haven't quite figured out whether the present situation, in the light of the changes introduced into life insurance policies and which we described in detail earlier, will be to their advantage or disadvantage. They will not take a step without being quite sure they are walking on firm ground, but when they finally do, they will put down new roots under whatever form of contract they draw up to suit their own best interests. Meanwhile, since the future belongs to god and because no one knows what tomorrow will bring, they will continue to consider as dead any insured person who has reached the age of eighty, that bird at least they have firmly grasped in their hand, and it only remains to be seen if tomorrow they can get two more to fall into the net. Some, however, propose that they should make the most of the current confusion in society, which stands more than ever between the devil and the deep blue sea, between scylla and charybdis, between a rock and a hard place, and that it might not be a bad idea to increase the age of actuarial death to eighty-five or even ninety. The reasoning of those who defend this change is as clear as water, they say that, by the time people reach such an age, not only do they have no relatives to look after them in time of need, indeed, any such relatives might be so old that it makes no odds anyway, they also suffer a real reduction in the value of their retirement pensions because of inflation and the rising cost of living, which means that they are often forced to interrupt payment of their premiums, thus giving insurance companies the best of motives to consider the respective contract null and void. That's inhuman, object some. Business is business, say the others. We will see how it all ends.

At this same hour, the maphia were also intently talking business. Perhaps because we were too thorough, as we unreservedly admit, the description we gave of the black tunnels through which the criminal organisation penetrated the world of funeral directors may have led some readers to wonder what kind of miserable maphia this is that it has no easier or more profitable ways of making money. Oh, but it has, and many and various they are, however, like any of its counterparts scattered throughout the world, skilled in balancing acts and in using tactics and strategies to best advantage, the local maphia did not merely rely on immediate gains, they were aiming higher than that, they had their eye on eternity, on neither more nor less than establishing, with the tacit agreement of families persuaded of the usefulness of euthanasia and with the blessing of politicians who would pretend to look the other way, an absolute monopoly on human deaths and burials, at the same time taking responsibility for keeping the nation's demographics at a level that was convenient for the country at any one time, turning the tap on and off, to use the image deployed before, or to use a more rigorously technical term, controlling the fluxometer. If they could not, at least in that initial phase, speed up or slow down procreation, it would at least be in their power to accelerate or delay journeys to the frontier, not the geographical one this time, but the eternal frontier. At the precise moment when we entered the room, the debate was focussed on how they could make optimum use of the work force that had been left idle since the return of death, and although there was no shortage of suggestions from around the table, some more radical than others, they ended up choosing one with a long proven track record and which would require no complicated mechanisms, namely, the protection business. The very next day, from north to south, in every part of the country, the offices of funeral directors saw two visitors come through their door, usually two men, sometimes a man and a woman, only rarely two women, who politely asked to speak to the manager, to whom they equally courteously explained that his business ran the risk of being attacked and even destroyed, either by bomb or fire, by activists from certain illegal groups of citizens who were demanding the inclusion of the right to eternal life in the universal declaration of human rights and who, frustrated in their desires, were now determined to vent their fury by letting the heavy hand of vengeance fall on innocent companies such as theirs, simply because they were the people who carried the corpses to their final resting place. We are told, said one of the emissaries, that these organised attacks, which could, if they met with any resistance, include the murder of the owner and the manager as well as their families, and if not them, then one or two employees, will start tomorrow, possibly here, possibly elsewhere, But what can I do, asked the poor manager, trembling,

Nothing, you can't do anything, but if you like, we can protect you, Yes, of course, if you can, There are a few conditions to be met, Whatever they are, please, protect me, The first is that you will not talk about this to anyone, not even to your wife, But I'm not married, It doesn't matter, not even to your mother, your grandmother or your aunt, My lips are sealed, Just as well, because, otherwise, you risk having them sealed for ever, And what about the other conditions, There's only one, to pay whatever we ask, Pay, We'll have to organise the protection operation, and that, dear sir, costs money, Ah, I understand, We could even protect the whole of humanity if it were prepared to pay the price, but meanwhile, since each age is always followed by another, we still live in hope, Hm, I see, How fortunate that you're so quick on the uptake, How much must I pay, It's written down on this piece of paper, That's a lot, It's the going rate, And is it per year or per month, Per week, But I don't have that kind of money, we funeral directors don't earn very much, You're lucky we're not asking you for what you, in your opinion, think your life is worth, Well, I only have one, And you could easily lose that, which is why we advise you to take good care of it, All right, I'll think about it, I need to talk to my partners, You have twenty-four hours, not a minute more, after that, we wash our hands of the matter, the responsibility will be yours alone, if anything should happen to you, we're pretty sure that the first time won't be fatal, and at that point, we'll come back and talk to you again, by then, of course, the price will have doubled and you'll have no option but to pay us whatever we ask, you can't imagine how implacable these citizens' groups demanding eternal life can be, All right, I'll pay, Four weeks in advance, please, Four weeks, Yours is an urgent case and, as we said before, it costs money to mount a protection operation, In cash or by cheque, In cash, cheques are for a different kind of transaction and for different sums of money, when it's best if the money doesn't pass directly from one hand to another. The manager went and opened the safe, counted out the notes and asked as he handed them over, Give me a receipt or some other document guaranteeing me protection, No receipt, no guarantee, you'll have to be content with our word of honour, Honour, Yes, honour, you can't imagine how thoroughly we honour our word, Where can I find you if I have a problem, Don't worry, we'll find you, I'll see you to the door, No, don't bother, we know the way, turn left after the store-room for coffins, past the make-up room, down the corridor, through reception and there's the street door, You won't get lost, We have a very keen sense of direction, we never get lost, for example, in five weeks' time, someone will come here to receive the next payment, How will I know it's the right person, You'll have no doubts when you see him, Goodbye, Yes, goodbye, no need to thank us.

Finally, last but not least, the catholic apostolic church of rome had many reasons to feel pleased with itself. Convinced from the start that the abolition of death could only be the work of the devil and that to help god fight the demon's works there is nothing more powerful than perserverance in prayer, they had set aside the virtue of modesty which, with no small effort and sacrifice, they usually cultivated, to congratulate themselves unreservedly on the success of the national campaign of prayer whose objective, remember, had been to ask the lord god to bring about the return of death as quickly as possible so as to save poor humanity from the worst horrors, end of quote. The prayers had taken nearly eight months to reach heaven, but when you think that it takes six months to reach the planet mars, then heaven, as you can imagine, must be much farther off, three thousand million light-years from earth, in round numbers. A black cloud, therefore, hung over the church's legitimate satisfaction. The theologians argued and failed to reach agreement on the reasons that had led god to order death's sudden return, without at least allowing time for the last rites to be given to the sixty-two thousand dying, who, deprived of the grace of the last sacrament, had expired in less time than it takes to say so. Worrying thoughts as to whether god had authority over death or if, on the contrary, death was above god in the hierarchy quietly gnawed away at the hearts and minds of that holy institution, where the bold affirmation that god and death were two sides of the same coin had come to be considered not so much heresy as an abominable sacrilege. At least that was what was really going on beneath the surface, whereas to others it seemed that the church's main preoccupation was their participation in the queen mother's funeral. Now that the sixty-two thousand ordinary dead were safely in their final resting place and no longer holding up the traffic in the city, it was time to bear the venerable lady, suitably enclosed in her lead coffin, to the royal pantheon. As the newspapers all agreed, it was the end of an era.

IT MAY BE THAT A VERY GENTEEL UPBRINGING, OF THE KIND THAT is becoming increasingly rare, along, perhaps, with the almost superstitious respect that the written word can instil into certain timid souls, has prevented readers, although they are more than justified in showing signs of ill-contained impatience, from interrupting this long digression and demanding to be told what death has been up to since the fateful night when she announced her return. Now given the important role that the eventide homes, the hospitals, the insurance companies, the maphia and the catholic church played in these extraordinary events, it seemed only fitting to explain in fulsome detail how they reacted to this sudden and dramatic turn of events, but   unless, of course, death, taking into account the enormous numbers of corpses that would have to be buried in the hours immediately following her announcement, had decided, in an unexpected and praiseworthy gesture of sympathy, to prolong her absence for a few more days in order to give life time to return to its old axes   other, newly dead people, that is, those who died during the first few days of the restoration of the old regime, would have been forced to join the unfortunates who had, for months, been hovering between here and there, and then, as is only logical, we would have been obliged to speak of those new deaths too. However, that is not what happened, Death was not so generous. The week-long pause, during which no one died and which, initially, created the illusion that nothing had, in fact, changed, came about simply because of the new rules governing the relationship between death and mortals, namely that everyone would receive prior warning that they still had a week to live until, shall we say, payment was due, a week in which to sort out their affairs, make a will, pay their back taxes and say goodbye to their family and to their closest friends. In theory, this seemed like a good idea, but practice would soon show that it was not. Imagine a person, the sort who enjoys splendid good health, who has never suffered from so much as a headache, an optimist both on principle and because he has clear and objective reasons for being so, and who, one morning, leaving his house on his way to work, meets his local and very helpful postman, who says, Lucky I caught you, mr so-and-so, I've got a letter for you, and the man receives in his hands a violet-coloured envelope to which he might pay no particular attention, after all, it's probably just more bumf from those direct marketing fellows, except that his name on the envelope is written in a strange hand, exactly like the writing on the famous facsimile published in the newspaper. If, at that moment, his heart gives a startled leap, if he's filled by a grim presentiment of some inevitable misfortune and he tries to refuse the letter, he won't be able to, it will be as if someone, gently holding his elbow, were guiding him down the steps to avoid slipping on a discarded banana skin, helping him round the corner so that he doesn't trip over his own feet. It will be pointless, too, trying to tear the envelope into pieces, because everyone knows that letters from death are, by definition, indestructible, not even an acetylene blowlamp at full blast could do away with them, and the ingenuous trick of pretending that he has dropped it would prove equally useless because the letter won't allow itself to fall, it will stay as if glued to his fingers, and even if, by some miracle, the impossible should happen, you can be sure that some goodhearted citizen would immediately pick it up and run after the person who was busily pretending not to have noticed and say, This letter is yours, I believe, it might be important, and the man would have to reply sadly, Yes, it is important, thank you very much for your pains. But that could only have happened at the beginning, when very few people knew that death was using the public postal service as a messenger for her funereal letters of notification. In a matter of days, the colour violet would become the most hated of all colours, even more so than black, despite the fact that black represented mourning, but then this is perfectly understandable when you consider that mourning is worn by the living, not the dead, although the latter do tend to be buried wearing black. Imagine, then, the bewilderment, fear and perplexity of that man setting off to work and seeing death suddenly step into his path in the shape of a postman who will definitely not ring twice, for, if he hadn't chanced to meet the addressee in the street, he would simply have put the letter through the relevant letter-box or slipped it under the door. The man is standing there, in the middle of the pavement, with his superb health, his solid head, so solid that even now, despite the terrible shock, it still doesn't ache, suddenly the world has ceased to belong to him or he to the world, they have merely been lent to each other for seven days and not a day longer, according to this violet-coloured letter he has just reluctantly opened, his eyes so full of tears that he can barely read what's written there, Dear sir, I regret to inform you that in a week your life will end, irrevocably and irremissibly. Please make the best use you can of the time remaining to you, yours faithfully, death. The signature has a lower-case d, which, as we know, acts, in some way, as its certificate of origin. The man hesitates, the postman called him mr so-and-so, which means, as we can see for ourselves, that he's of the male sex, the man wonders whether to go home and tell his family of this irrevocable sentence or if, on the contrary, he should bite back his tears and continue on his way to where his work awaits him and fill up what days remain to him, then feel able to ask, Death where is thy victory, knowing, however, that he will receive no reply, because death never replies, not because she doesn't want to, but because she doesn't know what to say in the face of the greatest of human sorrows.

This episode in the street, only possible in a small place where everyone knows everyone else, speaks volumes about the inconvenience of the communication system instituted by death for the termination of the temporary contract which we call life or existence. It could be seen as a display of sadistic cruelty, like so many others we see every day, but death has no need to be cruel, taking people's lives is more than enough. She simply hadn't thought it through. And now, absorbed as she must be in re-organising her support services after a long hiatus of more than seven months, she has neither eyes nor ears for the cries of despair and anguish uttered by the men and women who, one by one, are being warned of their imminent death, feelings of despair and anguish which, in some cases, are having precisely the opposite effect to the one she had foreseen, because the people condemned to disappear are not sorting out their affairs, they are not writing wills, they are not paying back taxes, and as for saying their farewells to family and close friends, they are leaving that to the last minute, which, of course, is not enough even for the most melancholy of farewells. Ill-informed about the true nature of death, whose other name is fate, the newspapers have outdone themselves in furious attacks on her, calling her pitiless, cruel, tyrannical, wicked, bloodthirsty, disloyal and treacherous, a vampire, the empress of evil, a dracula in skirts, the enemy of humankind, a murderess and, again, a serial killer, and there was even one weekly magazine, of the humorous kind, which, squeezing every ounce of sarcasm out of its copywriters, managed to come up with the term daughter-of-a-bitch. Fortunately, in some newspapers, good sense continues to reign. One of the most respected papers in the kingdom, the doyen of the national press, published a wise editorial in which it called for a frank and open dialogue with death, holding nothing back, with hand on heart and in a spirit of fraternity, always assuming, of course, that they could find out where she lived, her cave, her lair, her headquarters. Another paper suggested that the police authorities should investigate stationer's shops and paper manufacturers, because human users of violet-coloured envelopes, if ever there were any, and they would always have been very few, would be sure to have changed their epistolary tastes in view of recent events, and it would thus be as easy as pie to catch the macabre customer when she turned up to refresh her supplies. Another newspaper, a bitter rival of the latter, was quick to describe this idea as both crass and stupid, because only an arrant fool could think that death, who, as everyone knew, was a skeleton draped in a sheet, would set out, bony heels clattering along the pavement, to mail her letters. Not wishing to lag behind the press, the television advised the interior minister to have policemen guard post boxes and pillar boxes, apparently forgetting that the first letter addressed to the director-general of television had appeared in his office when the door was double-locked and no window-panes broken. Floor, walls and ceilings revealed not a crack, not even one tiny enough to slip a razor-blade through. Perhaps it really was possible to persuade death to show more compassion towards the poor unfortunates condemned to die, but to do that, they would have to find her and no one knew how or where.

It was then that a forensic scientist, well informed about everything that related, directly or indirectly, to his profession, had the idea of inviting over a celebrated foreign expert in the reconstruction of faces from skulls, this expert, basing himself on representations of death in old paintings and engravings, especially those showing her bare cranium, would try to replace any missing flesh, restore the eyes to their sockets, add, in just proportions, hair, eyelashes and eyebrows, as well as appropriate touches of colour to the cheeks, until before him appeared a perfect, finished head of which a thousand photographic copies would then be made so that the same number of investigators could carry it in their wallets to compare with the many women they would see. The trouble was that, when the foreign expert had concluded his work, only someone with a very untrained eye would have said that the three chosen skulls were identical, and this obliged the investigators to work with not just one photograph, but three, which would obviously hinder the death-hunt, as the operation had, rather ambitiously, been called. Only one thing had been proved beyond doubt, and about which even the most rudimentary iconography, the most complicated nomenclature, and the most abstruse symbolism had all been correct. Death, in her features, attributes and characteristics, was unmistakably a woman. As you will doubtless remember, the eminent graphologist who studied death's first letter had clearly reached the same conclusion when he referred to the writer of the letter as its authoress, but that might have been pure habit, given that, with the exception of a very few languages, which, for some unknown reason, opt for the masculine or the neuter, death has always been a person of the female gender. Now we have given this information before, but, lest you forget, it would be as well to insist on the fact that the three faces, all of them female and all of them young, did differ from each other in certain ways, despite the clear similarities that everyone saw in them. The existence of three different deaths, for example, working in shifts, was simply not credible, so two of them would have to be excluded, although, just to complicate matters still further, it might well be that the skeletal model of the real and true death did not correspond to any of the three who had been selected. It was, as the saying goes, a question of firing a shot in the dark and hoping that benevolent chance had time to place the target in the bullet's path.

The investigation began, as it had to, in the archives of the official identification service in which were gathered photographs of all the country's inhabitants, both indigenous and foreign, classified and ordered according to certain basic characteristics, the dolichocephalic to one side, the brachycephalic to the other. The results were disappointing. At first, of course, since, as we said before, the models chosen for the facial reconstruction had been taken from old engravings and paintings, no one really hoped to find the humanised image of death in these modern identification systems, instituted just over a century ago, but, on the other hand, bearing in mind that death has always existed and since there seems no reason to suppose that she would have needed to change her face over the ages, and not forgetting that it must be difficult for her to carry out her work properly and safe from suspicion while living in clandestinity, it is therefore perfectly logical to accept the hypothesis that she might have put herself down in the civil registry under a false name, for as we know all too well, nothing is impossible for death. Whatever the truth of the matter, the fact is that, despite asking for help from those gifted in information technology and data exchange, the investigators found not a single photograph of any identifiable woman who looked anything like the three virtual images of death. As had already been foreseen, there was, then, no alternative but to return to the classic investigatory methods, to the policemanly craft of piecing together snippets of information and sending forth those one thousand agents so that, by going from house to house, from shop to shop, from office to office, from factory to factory, from restaurant to restaurant, from bar to bar, and even visiting those places reserved for the onerous exercise of sex, they could inspect all the women in the land, excluding adolescents and those of mature or advanced years, because the three photographs they had in their pocket made it quite clear that death, if ever she were found, would be a woman of about thirty-six and very beautiful indeed. According to the model they had been given, any of them could have been death, although none of them was. After enormous effort, after trudging miles and miles along streets, roads and paths, after going up flights of stairs which, placed end to end, would have carried them up to the skies, the agents managed to identify two of these women, who only differed from the existing photographs in the archives because they had benefitted from cosmetic surgery, which, by an astonishing coincidence, by a strange happenstance, had emphasised the similarities of their faces to the reconstructed faces of the models. However, a meticulous examination of their respective biographies ruled out, with no margin for error, any possibility that they had once dedicated themselves, even in their spare time, to the deadly activities of death, either professionally or as mere amateurs. As for the third woman, identified only from family albums, she had died the previous year. By a simple process of elimination, someone who had been the victim of death could not also be death. And needless to say, while the investigations were going on, and they lasted some weeks, the violet-coloured envelopes continued to arrive at the homes of their addressees. It was clear that death would not budge from her agreement with humanity.

Naturally, one must ask if the government was merely standing by and impassively watching the daily drama being lived out by the country's ten million inhabitants. The answer is twofold, affirmative on the one hand and negative on the other. Affirmative, although only in rather relative terms, because dying is, after all, the most normal and ordinary thing in life, a purely routine fact, an episode in the endless legacy passed from parents to children, at least since adam and eve, and world governments would do enormous harm to the public's precarious peace of mind if they declared three days of national mourning every time some poor old man died in a home for the destitute. And negative because it would be impossible, even if you had a heart of stone, to remain indifferent to the palpable fact that the week's notice given by death had taken on the proportions of a real collective calamity, not just for the average of three hundred people at whose door ill luck came knocking each day, but also for the people who remained, neither more nor less than nine million nine hundred and ninety-nine thousand and seven hundred people of all ages, fortunes and conditions, who, each morning when they woke from a night tormented by the most terrible nightmares, saw the sword of damocles hanging by a thread over their head. As for the three hundred inhabitants who had received the fateful violet-coloured letter, responses to the implacable sentence varied, as is only natural, depending on the character of each individual. As well as those people mentioned above who, driven by a twisted idea of revenge to which one could quite rightly apply the neologism preposthumous, decided to abandon their civic and familial duties by not writing a will or paying their back taxes, there were many who, acting on a highly corrupt interpretation of the horatian carpe diem, squandered what little life was left to them by giving themselves over to reprehensible orgies of sex, drugs and alcohol, thinking perhaps that by falling into such wild excesses, they might bring down upon their own heads some fatal stroke or, if not, a divine thunderbolt which, by killing them there and then would snatch them from the grasp of death proper, thus playing a trick on death that might well make her change her ways. Others, stoical, dignified and courageous, went for the radical option of suicide, believing that they, too, would be teaching a lesson in manners to the power of thanatos, delivering what we used to call a verbal slap in the face, of the sort that, in accordance with the honest convictions of the time, would be all the more painful if it had its origin in the ethical and moral arena and not in some primitive desire for physical revenge. All these attempts failed, of course, apart, that is, from those stubborn people who reserved their suicide for the last day of the deadline. A masterly move, to which death could find no answer.

To its credit, the first institution to get a real sense of the mood of the people in general was the catholic apostolic church of rome, to which, since we live in an age dominated by the boom in the use of acronyms in day-to-day communications, both private and public, it might be a good idea to give the easier abbreviation of cacor. It is also true that you would have had to be stone-blind not to notice how, almost from one moment to the next, the churches filled up with distraught people in search of some word of hope, some consolation, a balm, an analgesic, a spiritual tranquilliser. People who, until then, had lived in the consciousness that death was inevitable and that there was no possible escape, but thinking at the same time, since there were so many other people doomed to die, that only by some real stroke of bad luck would their turn ever come around, those same people now spent their time peering from behind the curtains, waiting for the postman or trembling when they returned home, where the dreaded violet-coloured letter, worse than a bloody monster with jaws gaping, might be lurking behind the door, ready to leap out at them. The churches did not stop work for a moment, the long queues of contrite sinners, constantly refreshed like factory assembly lines, wound twice round the central nave. The confessors on duty never stopped, sometimes they were distracted by fatigue, at others their attention was suddenly caught by some scandalous detail, but in the end they simply handed out a pro forma penance, so many our fathers, so many ave marias, and then muttered a hasty absolution. In the brief interval between one confessee leaving and the next confessant kneeling down, the confessors would grab a bite of the chicken sandwich that would be their lunch, meanwhile vaguely imagining some compensatory delight for supper. Sermons were invariably on the subject of death as the only way into the heavenly paradise, where, it was said, no one ever entered alive, and the preachers, in their eagerness to console, did not hesitate to resort to the highest forms of rhetoric and to the lowest tricks in the catechism to convince their terrified parishioners that they could, after all, consider themselves more fortunate than their ancestors, because death had given them enough time to prepare their souls with a view to ascending into eden. There were some priests, however, who, trapped in the malodorous gloom of the confessional, had to screw up their courage, god knows at what cost, because they, too, that very morning, had received the violet-coloured envelope, and so had more than enough reason to doubt the emollient virtues of what they were saying.

The same was happening with the mental therapists that the health minister, hastening to imitate the therapeutic aid given by the church, had despatched to bring succour to the most desperate. It was not infrequent for a psychiatrist, when counselling a patient that crying would be the best way to relieve the pain tormenting him, to burst into convulsive sobs himself when he remembered that he, too, might be the recipient of an identical envelope in the next day's post. Both psychiatrist and patient would end the session bawling their eyes out, embraced by the same misfortune, but with the therapist thinking that if a misfortune did befall him, he would still have seven days to live, one hundred and ninety-two hours. A few little orgies of sex, drugs and alcohol, which he had heard were being organised, would ease his passage into the next world, although, of course, you then ran the risk that such excesses might only make you miss this world all the more intensely when you were up there on your ethereal throne.

ACCORDING TO THE WISDOM OF THE NATIONS, THERE IS AN exception to every rule, even rules that would normally be considered utterly inviolable, as for example, those regarding the sovereignty of death, to which, by definition, there never could be an exception, however absurd, and yet it really must be true because, as it happened, one violet-coloured letter was returned to sender. Some will object that such a thing is impossible, that death, being ubiquitous, cannot therefore be in any one particular place, from which one can deduce the impossibility, both material and metaphysical, of locating and defining what we normally understand by the word sender, or, in the meaning intended here, the place from which the letter came. Others will also object, albeit less speculatively, that, since a thousand policemen have been looking for death for weeks on end, scouring the entire country, house by house, with a fine-tooth comb, as if in search of an elusive louse highly skilled in evasive tactics, and have still found neither hide nor hair of her, it is as clear as day that if no explanation has yet been given as to how death's letters reach the mail, we are certainly not going to be told by what mysterious channels the returned letter has managed to reach her hands. We humbly recognise that our explanations about this and much more have been sadly lacking, we confess that we are unable to provide explanations that will satisfy those demanding them, unless, taking advantage of the reader's credulity and leaping over the respect owed to the logic of events, we were to add further unrealities to the congenital unreality of this fable, now we realise that such faults seriously undermine our story's credibility, however, none of this, we repeat, none of this means that the violet-coloured letter to which we referred was not returned to its sender. Facts are facts, and this fact, whether you like it or not, is of the irrefutable kind. There can be no better proof of this than the image of death before us now, sitting on a chair while wrapped in her sheet, and with a look of blank amazement on the orography of her bony face. She eyes the violet envelope suspiciously, studies it to see if it bears any of the comments postmen usually write on envelopes in such cases, for example, returned, not known at this address, addressee gone away leaving no forwarding address or date of return, or simply, dead, How stupid of me, she muttered, how could he have died if the letter that should have killed him came back unopened. She had thought these last words without giving them much importance, but she immediately summoned them up again and repeated them out loud, in a dreamy tone of voice, Came back unopened. You don't need to be a postman to know that coming back is not the same thing as being sent back, that coming back could merely mean that the violet-coloured letter failed to reach its destination, that at some point along the way something happened to make it retrace its steps and return whence it had come. Letters can only go where they're taken, they don't have legs or wings, and, as far as we know, they're not endowed with their own initiative, if they were, we're sure that they would refuse to carry the terrible news of which they're so often the bearers. Like this news of mine, thought death impartially, telling someone that they're going to die on a particular date is the worst possible news, it's like spending long years on death row and then having the jailer come up to you and say, Here's the letter, prepare yourself. The odd thing is that all the other letters from the last batch were safely delivered to their addressees, and if this one wasn't, it can only have been because of some chance event, for just as there have been cases of a love letter, god alone knows with what consequences, taking five years to reach an addressee who lived only two blocks and less than a quarter of an hour's walk away, it could be that this letter passed from one conveyor belt to another without anyone noticing and then returned to its point of departure like someone who, lost in the desert, has nothing more to go on than the trail he left behind him. The solution would be to send it again, said death to the scythe that was next to her, leaning against the white wall. One wouldn't expect a scythe to respond, and this one proved no exception. Death went on, If I'd sent you, with your taste for expeditious methods, the matter would have been resolved, but times have changed a lot lately, and one has to update the means and the systems one uses, to keep up with the new technologies, by using e-mail, for example, I've heard tell that it's the most hygienic way, one that does away with inkblots and finger-prints, besides which it's fast, you just open up outlook express on microsoft and it's gone, the difficulty would be having to work with two separate archives, one for those who use computers and another for those who don't, anyway, we've got plenty of time to think about it, they're always coming out with new models and new designs, with new improved tech-nologies, perhaps I'll try it some day, but until then, I'll continue to write with pen, paper and ink, it has the charm of tradition, and tradition counts for a lot when it comes to dying. Death stared hard at the violet-coloured envelope, made a gesture with her right hand, and the letter vanished. So now we know that, contrary to what so many thought, death does not take her letters to the post office.

On the table is a list of two hundred and ninety-eight names, rather fewer than usual, one hundred and fifty-two men and one hundred and forty-six women, and the same number of violet-coloured envelopes and sheets of paper are ready for the next mailing, or death-by-post. Death added to the list the name on the letter that had been returned to sender, underlined it and replaced her pen in the pen holder. If she had any nerves at all, we could say that she felt slightly excited, and with good reason. She had lived for far too long to consider the return of the letter unimportant. It's easy enough to understand, it takes very little imagination to see why death's workplace is probably the dullest of all those created since cain killed abel, an incident for which god bears all the blame. Since that first deplorable incident, which, from the moment the world began, demonstrated the difficulties of family life, and right up until the present day, the process has remained unchanged for centuries and centuries and more centuries, repetitive, unceasing, uninterrupted, unbroken, varying only in the many ways of passing from life to non-life, but basically always the same because the result was always the same. The fact is that whoever was meant to die died. And now, remarkably, a letter signed by death, written in her own hand, a letter warning of someone's irrevocable and unpostponable end, had been returned to sender, to this cold room where the author and signatory of the letter sits, wrapped in the melancholy shroud that is her historic uniform, the hood over her head, as she ponders what has happened, meanwhile drumming on the desk with the bones of her fingers, or the fingers of her bones. She's slightly surprised to find herself hoping that the letter will be returned again, that the envelope will carry, for example, a message denying all knowledge of the addressee's whereabouts, because that really would be a new experience for someone who has always managed to find us wherever we were hidden, if, in that childish way, we thought we might escape her. However, she doesn't really believe that the supposed absence will be marked on the back of the envelope, here the archives are updated automatically with every gesture or movement we make, with every step we take, every change of house, status, profession, habit or custom, if we smoke or don't smoke, if we eat a lot or a little or nothing, if we're active or indolent, if we have a headache or indigestion, if we suffer from constipation or diarrhoea, if our hair falls out or we get cancer, if it's a yes, a no or a maybe, all she will have to do is open the drawer of the alphabetical file, look for the corresponding folder, and there it will all be. And it shouldn't astonish us in the least if, at the very moment we were reading our own personal file, we saw instantaneously recorded there the sudden pang of anxiety that froze us. Death knows everything about us, and that perhaps is why she's sad. If it's true that she doesn't smile, this is only because she has no lips, and this anatomical lesson tells us that, contrary to what the living may believe, a smile is not a matter of teeth. There are those who say, with a sense of humour that owes more to a lack of taste than it does to the macabre, that she wears a kind of permanent, fixed grin, but that isn't true, what she wears is a grimace of pain, because she's constantly pursued by the memory of the time when she had a mouth, and her mouth a tongue, and her tongue saliva. With a brief sigh, she took up a sheet of paper and began writing the first letter of the day, Dear madam, I regret to inform you that in a week your life will end, irrevocably and irremissibly. Please make the best use you can of the time remaining to you, yours faithfully, death. Two hundred and ninety-eight sheets of paper, two hundred and ninety-eight envelopes, two hundred and ninety-eight names removed from the list, this is not exactly a killingly hard job, but the fact is that when she reaches the end, death is exhausted. Making that gesture with her right hand with which we're already familiar, she despatched the two hundred and ninety-eight letters, then, folding her bony arms on the desk, she rested her head on them, not in order to sleep, because death doesn't sleep, but in order to rest. When, half an hour later, once recovered from her tiredness, she raised her head, the letter that had been returned to sender and sent again was back, right there before her empty, astonished eye sockets.

If death had dreamed hopefully of some surprise to distract her from the boredom of routine, she was well served. Here was that surprise, and it could hardly be bettered. The first time the letter was returned could have been put down to a mere accident along the way, a castor come off its axle, a lubrication problem, a sky-blue letter in a hurry to arrive that had pushed its way to the front, in short, one of those unexpected things that happen inside machines, or, indeed, inside the human body, and which can throw out even the most exact calculations. The fact that it had been returned twice was quite different, it clearly showed that there was an obstacle at some point along the road that should have taken it straight to the home of the addressee, an obstacle that sent the letter rebounding back to where it had come from. In the first instance, given that the return had taken place on the day after it had been sent, it was still possible that the postman, having failed to find the person to whom the letter should have been delivered, instead of putting the letter through the letter-box or under the door, had returned it to the sender, but omitted to give a reason. All this was pure supposition, of course, but it could explain what had happened. Now, however, things were different. Between coming and going, the letter had taken less than half an hour, probably much less, for it was there on the desk when death raised her head from the rather hard resting-place of her forearms, that is from the cubit and the radius, which are intertwined for that very purpose. A strange, mysterious, incomprehensible force appeared to be resisting the death of that person, even though the date of his demise had been fixed, as it had for everyone, from the day of his birth. It's impossible, said death to the silent scythe, no one in this world or beyond has ever had more power than I have, I'm death, all else is nothing. She got up from her chair and went over to the filing cabinet, from which she returned with the suspect file. There was no doubt about it, the name agreed with that on the envelope, so did the address, the person's profession was given as cellist and the space for civil status was blank, a sign that he was neither married, widowed or divorced, because in death's files the status of bachelor is never recorded, well, you can imagine how silly it would be for a child to be born, an index card filled out, and to note down, not his profession, because he wouldn't yet know what his vocation would be, but that the new-born's civil status was bachelor. As for the age given on the card that death is holding in her hand, we can see that the cellist is forty-nine years old. Now, if we needed proof of the impeccable workings of death's archives, we will have it now, when, in a tenth of a second, or even less, before our own incredulous eyes, the number forty-nine is replaced by fifty. Today is the birthday of the cellist whose name is on the card, he should be receiving flowers not a warning that in a week's time he'll be dead. Death got up again, walked around the room a few times, stopped twice as she passed the scythe, opened her mouth as if to speak or ask an opinion or issue an order, or simply to say that she felt confused, upset, which, we must say, is hardly surprising when we think how long she has done this job without, until now, ever having been shown any disrespect from the human flock of which she is the sovereign shepherdess. It was then that death had the grim presentiment that the incident might be even more serious than had at first seemed. She sat down at her desk and started to leaf back through last week's list of the dead. On the first list of names from yesterday, and contrary to what she had expected, she saw that the cellist's name was missing. She continued to turn the pages, one, then another, then another and another, one more, and only on the eighth list did she find his name. She had erroneously thought that the name would be on yesterday's list, but now she found herself before an unprecedented scandal: someone who should have been dead two days ago was still alive. And that wasn't the worst of it. The wretched cellist, who, ever since his birth, had been marked out to die a young man of only forty-nine summers, had just brazenly entered his fiftieth year, thus bringing into disrepute destiny, fate, fortune, the horoscope, luck and all the other powers that devote themselves by every possible means, worthy and unworthy, to thwarting our very human desire to live. They were all utterly discredited. And how am I going to put right a mistake that could never have happened, when a case like this has no precedents, when nothing like it was foreseen in the regulations, thought death, especially when the man was supposed to have died at forty-nine and not at fifty, which is the age he is now. Poor death was clearly beside herself, distraught, and would soon start beating her head against the wall out of sheer distress. In all these thousands of centuries of continuous activity, there had never been a single operational failure, and now, just when she had introduced something new into the classic relationship between mortals and their one and only causa mortis, her hard-won reputation had been dealt the severest of blows. What should I do, she asked, what if the fact that he didn't die when he should have has placed him beyond my jurisdiction, how on earth am I going to get out of this fix. She looked at the scythe, her companion in so many adventures and massacres, but the scythe ignored her, it never responded, and now, oblivious to everything, as if weary of the world, it was resting its worn, rusty blade against the white wall. That was when death came up with her great idea, People say that there's never a one without a two, never a two without a three, and that three is lucky because it's the number god chose, but let's see if it's true. She waved her right hand, and the letter that had been returned twice vanished again. Within two minutes it was back. There it was, in the same place as before. The postman hadn't put it under the door, he hadn't rung the bell, and there it was.

Obviously, we have no reason to feel sorry for death. Our complaints have been far too numerous and far too justified for us to express for her a pity which at no moment in the past did she have the delicacy to show to us, even though she knew better than anyone how we loathed the obstinacy with which she always, whatever the cost, got her own way. And yet, for a brief moment, what we have before us is more like an image of desolation than the sinister figure who, according to a few unusually perspicacious individuals lying on their deathbed, appears at the foot of the bed at our final hour to make a gesture similar to the one she makes when she despatches the letters, except that the gesture means come here, not go away. Due to some strange optical phenomenon, real or virtual, death seems much smaller now, as if her bones had shrunk, or perhaps she was always like that, and it's our eyes, wide with fear, that make her look like a giant. Poor death. It makes us feel like going over and putting a hand on her hard shoulder and whispering a few words of sympathy in her ear, or, rather, in the place where her ear once was, underneath the parietal. Don't get upset, madam death, such things are always happening, we human beings, for example, have long experience of disappointments, failures and frustrations, and yet we don't give up, remember the old days when you used to snatch us away in the flower of our youth without a flicker of sadness or compassion, think of today when, with equal hardness of heart, you continue to do the same to people who lack all the necessities of life, we've probably been waiting to see who would tire first, you or us, I understand your distress, the first defeat is the hardest, then you get used to it, but please don't take it the wrong way when I say that I hope it won't be the last, I say this not out of any spirit of revenge, well, it would be a pretty poor revenge, wouldn't it, rather like sticking my tongue out at the executioner who's about to chop off my head, although, to be honest, we human beings can't do much more than stick out our tongue at the executioner about to chop off our head, that must be why I can't wait to see how you're going to get out of the mess you're in, with this letter that keeps coming and going and that cellist who can't die at forty-nine because he's just turned fifty. Death made an impatient gesture, roughly shrugged off the fraternal hand we had placed on her shoulder and got up from her chair. She seemed taller now, larger, a proper dame death, capable of making the earth tremble beneath her feet, with her shroud dragging behind her, throwing up clouds of smoke with each step she takes. Death is angry. It's high time we stuck out our tongues at her.

APART FROM A FEW RARE INSTANCES, AS WITH THOSE UNUSUALLY perspicacious people whom we mentioned before, who, as they lay dying, spotted her at the foot of the bed in the classic garb of a ghost swathed in a white sheet or, as appears to have happened with proust, in the guise of a fat woman dressed in black, death is usually very discreet and prefers not to be noticed, especially if circumstances oblige her to go out into the street. There is a widely held belief that since death, as some like to say, is one side of a coin of which god is the reverse, she must, like him, by her very nature, be invisible. Well, it isn't quite like that. We are reliable witnesses to the fact that death is a skeleton wrapped in a sheet, that she lives in a chilly room accompanied by a rusty old scythe that never replies to questions, and is surrounded only by cobwebs and a few dozen filing cabinets with large drawers stuffed with index cards. One can understand, therefore, why death wouldn't want to appear before people in that get-up, firstly, for reasons of personal pride, secondly, so that the poor passers-by wouldn't die of fright when, on turning a corner, they came face to face with those large empty eye-sockets. In public, of course, death makes herself invisible, but not in private, at the critical moment, as attested by the writer marcel proust and those other unusually perspicacious people. The case of god is different. However hard he tried, he could never manage to make himself visible to human eyes and not because he can't, since for him nothing is impossible, it's simply that

134

he wouldn't know what face to wear when introducing himself to the beings he supposedly created and who probably wouldn't recognise him anyway. There are those who say we're very fortunate that god chooses not to appear before us, because compared with the shock we would get were such a thing to happen, our fear of death would be mere child's play. Besides, all the many things that have been said about god and about death are nothing but stories, and this is just another one.

Anyway, death decided to go into town. She took off the sheet, which was all she was wearing, carefully folded it up and hung it over the back of the chair where we have seen her sitting. Apart from the chair and the desk, apart, too, from the filing cabinets and the scythe, the room is otherwise bare, save for that narrow door which leads we know not where. Since it appears to be the only way out, it would be logical to think that death will pass through there in order to go into town, however, this proves not to be the case. Without the sheet, death seemed to lose height, she's probably, at most, in human measurements, a metre sixty-six or sixty-seven, and when naked, without a thread of clothing on, she seems still smaller, almost a tiny adolescent skeleton. No one would say that this is the same death who so violently rejected our hand on her shoulder when, moved by misplaced feelings of pity, we tried to offer solace in her sadness. There really is nothing in the world as naked as a skeleton. In life, it walks around doubly clothed, first by the flesh concealing it, then by the clothes with which said flesh likes to cover itself, if it hasn't removed them to take a bath or to engage in other more pleasurable activities. Reduced to what she really is, the half-dismantled scaffolding of someone who long ago ceased to exist, all that remains for death now is to disappear. And that is precisely what is happening to her, from her head to her toes. Before our astonished eyes, her bones are losing substance and solidity, her edges are growing blurred, what was solid is becoming gaseous, spreading everywhere like a tenuous mist, it's as if her skeleton were evaporating, now she's just a vague sketch through which one can see the indifferent scythe, and suddenly death is no longer there, she was and now she isn't, or she is, but we can't see her, or not even that, she simply passed straight through the ceiling of the subterranean room, through the enormous mass of earth above, and set off, as she had privately determined to do when the violet-coloured letter was returned to her for the third time. We know where she's going. She can't kill the cellist, but she wants to see him, to have him there before her gaze, to touch him without his realising. She's convinced that she will one day find a way of getting rid of him without breaking too many rules, but meanwhile she will find out who he is, this man whom death's warnings could not reach, what powers he has, if any, or if, like an innocent fool, he continues to live, never once thinking that he ought to be dead. Shut up in this cold room with no windows and only a narrow door leading who knows where, we hadn't noticed how quickly time passes. It's three o'clock in the morning, and death must already be in the cellist's house.

So it is. One of the things that death finds most tiring is the effort it takes to stop herself seeing everything everywhere simultaneously. In that respect, too, she is very like god. For although the fact doesn't appear amongst the verifiable data of human sensorial experience, we have been accustomed to believe, ever since we were children, that god and death, those supreme eminences, are everywhere always, that is, omni-present, a word, like so many others, made up of space and time. It's highly likely, however, that when we think this, and perhaps even more so when we put it into words, considering how easily words leave our mouths, we have no clear idea what we mean. It's easy enough to say that god is everywhere and that death is everywhere too, but we don't seem to realise that if they really are everywhere, then, inevitably, in all the infinite parts in which they find themselves, they see everything there is to see. Since god is duty-bound to be, at one and the same time, everywhere in the whole universe, because otherwise there would be no point in his having created it, it would be ridiculous to expect him to take a particular interest in little planet earth, which, and this is something that has not perhaps occurred to anyone else, he may know by some other completely different name, but death, the same death which, as we said a few pages earlier, is bound exclusively to the human race, doesn't take her eyes off us for a minute, so much so that even those who are not yet due to die feel her gaze pursuing them constantly. This will give some idea of the herculean effort death was obliged to make on the rare occasions when, for one reason or another, throughout our shared history, she has had to reduce her perceptive abilities down to our human level, that is, to see just one thing at a time, to be in only one place at any one moment. In the particular case that concerns us today, that is the only way to explain why she has not yet managed to get any further than the hallway of the cellist's apartment. With each step she takes, and we only call it a step to help the reader's imagination, not because she actually requires legs and feet to move, death has to struggle hard to repress the expansive tendency inherent in her nature, and which, if given free rein, would immediately explode and shatter the precarious and unstable unity so painfully achieved. The cellist who failed to receive the violet-coloured letter lives in the kind of apartment that could be categorised as comfortable, and therefore more suited to a petit bourgeois with limited horizons than to a disciple of euterpe. You enter via a corridor where, in the darkness, you can just about make out five doors, one at the far end, which, just so that we don't have to repeat ourselves, gives access to the bathroom, with two doors to either side of it. The first door on the left as you go in, which is where death decides to begin her inspection, opens onto a small dining room which shows every sign of being little used, and in turn leads into an even smaller kitchen, equipped only with the basics. From there you go back out into the corridor, immediately opposite a door which death didn't even need to touch to know that it wasn't used, that is, it neither opens nor closes, a turn of phrase which defies the simple facts, for a door of which you can say that it neither opens nor closes is merely a closed door that you cannot open, or as it is also known, a condemned door. Death, of course, could walk straight through it and through whatever lay behind it, but even though she is still invisible to ordinary eyes, it nevertheless took a great deal of effort to form and define herself into a more or less human shape, although, as we mentioned before, not to the extent of having legs and feet, and she is not prepared now to run the risk of relaxing and becoming dispersed in the wooden interior of a door or the wardrobe full of clothes that is doubtless on the other side. So death continued along the corridor to the first proper door on the right and, going through that door, she found herself in the music room, for what other name could you give to a room where you find an open piano and a cello, a music stand bearing robert schumann's three fantasy pieces opus seventy-three, as death is able to read in the pale orangish light from a street lamp pouring in through the two windows, as well as, here and there, piles of sheet music, and, of course, the tall shelves of books where literature appears to live alongside music in the most perfect harmony, she who was once the daughter of ares and aphrodite, but is now the science of chords. Death caressed the strings of the cello, softly ran her fingers over the keys of the piano, but only she could have heard the sound of the instruments, a long, grave moan followed by a brief bird-like trill, both inaudible to human ears, but clear and precise to someone who had long ago learned to interpret the meaning of sighs. There, in the room next door, must be where the man sleeps. The door is open, the darkness, although it is darker there than in the music room, nevertheless reveals a bed and the shape of someone lying there. Death advances, crosses the threshold, but then stops, hesitant, when she feels the presence of two living beings in the room. Aware of certain facts of life, although, naturally enough, not from personal experience, it occurred to death that perhaps the man had company and that another person was sleeping beside him, someone to whom she had not yet sent a violet-coloured letter, but who, in this apartment, shared the shelter of the same sheets and the warmth of the same blanket. She went closer, almost brushing, if one can say such a thing of death, the bedside table, and saw that the man was alone. However, on the other side of the bed, curled up on the carpet like a ball of wool, slept a medium-sized dog with dark, probably black hair. As far as death could remember, this was the first time she had found herself thinking that, given that she dealt only with human deaths, this animal was beyond the reach of her symbolic scythe, that her power could not touch him however lightly, and that this sleeping dog would also become immortal, although who knows for how long, if his death, the other death, the one in charge of all other living beings, animal and vegetable, were to absent herself as she had done, giving someone the perfect reason to begin a book with the words The next day no dog died. The man stirred, perhaps he was dreaming, perhaps he was still playing the three schumann pieces and had played a wrong note, a cello isn't like a piano, on the piano, the notes are always in the same places, underneath each key, while on the cello they're scattered along the length of the strings, and you have to go and look for them, to pin them down, find the exact point, move the bow at just the right angle and with just the right pressure, so nothing could be easier than to hit one or two wrong notes while you're sleeping. As death leaned forward to get a better look at the man's face, she had an absolutely brilliant idea, it occurred to her that the index cards in her archive should each bear a photograph of the person in question, not an ordinary photograph, but one so scientifically advanced that, just as the details of people's lives were continually and automatically being updated, so their image would change with passing time, from the red and wrinkled babe in arms to today, when we wonder if we really are the person we were, or if, with each passing hour, some genie of the lamp is not constantly replacing us with someone else. The man stirred again, it seems as if he's about to wake, but no, his breathing returns to its normal rhythm, the same thirteen breaths a minute, his left hand rests on his heart as if he were listening to the beats, an open note for diastole, a closed note for systole, while the right hand, palm uppermost and fingers slightly curved, seems to be waiting for another hand to clasp it. The man looks older than his fifty years, or perhaps not older, perhaps he's merely tired, or sad, but this we will only know when he opens his eyes. He has lost some of his hair, and much of what remains is already white. He's a perfectly ordinary man, neither ugly nor handsome. Looking at him now, lying on his back, his striped pyjama jacket exposed by the turned-down sheet, no one would think he was first cellist in one of the city's symphony orchestras, that his life runs between the magical lines of the pentagram, perhaps, who knows, searching for the deep heart of the music, pause, sound, systole, diastole. Still annoyed by the failure of the state's postal communications system, but not as irritated as when she arrived, death looks at the man's sleeping face and thinks vaguely that he should be dead, that the heart being protected by his left hand should be still and empty, frozen for ever in that last contraction. She came to see this man and now that she has, there is nothing sufficiently special about him to explain why the violet-coloured letter was returned three times, the best she can do after this is to return to the cold, subterranean room whence she came and to discover a way of resolving this wretched stroke of fate that has turned this scraper of cellos into a survivor of himself. Death used those two aggressive words, wretched and scraper in order to rouse her now dwindling sense of annoyance, but the attempt failed. The man sleeping there is not to blame for what happened with the violet-coloured letter, nor can he have even the remotest idea that he is living a life that should no longer be his, that if things had turned out as they should, he would have been dead and buried now for a good week, and that his dog would be running around the city like a mad thing, looking for his master, or else sitting, without eating or drinking, at the entrance to the building, waiting for him to come back. For a moment, death let herself go, expanding out as far as the walls, filling that whole room and flowing into the room next door, where a part of her stopped to look at the sheet music open on a chair, it was suite number six opus one thousand and twelve in d major by johann sebastian bach, composed in köthen, and she didn't need to be able to read music to know that it had been written, like beethoven's ninth symphony, in the key of joy, of unity between men, of friendship and of love. Then something extraordinary happened, something unimaginable, death fell to her knees, for she had a body now, which is why she had knees and legs and feet and arms and hands, and a face which she covered with her hands, and shoulders, which, for some reason, were shaking, she can't be crying, you can't expect that from someone who, wherever she goes, has always left a trail of tears behind her, without one of those tears shed being hers. Just as she was, neither visible nor invisible, neither skeleton nor woman, she leapt, light as air, to her feet and went back into the bedroom. The man had not moved. Death thought, There's nothing more for me to do here, I'm leaving, it was hardly worth coming really just to see a man and a dog asleep, perhaps they're dreaming about each other, the man about the dog, the dog about the man, the dog dreaming that it's morning already and that he's laying his head down beside the man's head, the man dreaming that it's morning already and that his left arm is grasping the soft, warm body of the dog and holding it close to his breast. Beside the wardrobe blocking the door that would otherwise open onto the corridor is a small sofa where death has gone to sit. She hadn't intended to, but she went to sit down in that corner anyway, perhaps remembering how cold it would be at that hour in her subterranean archive room. Her eyes are on a level now with the man's head, she can see his profile clearly silhouetted against the backdrop of that vague, orangey light coming in through the window and she repeats to herself that there's no rational reason for staying there, but she immediately argues with herself that there is, that there is a reason, and a very good one, because this is the only house in the city, in the country, in the whole world, where someone is infringing the harshest of nature's laws, the law that imposes on us both life and death, which did not ask if you wanted to live, and which will not ask if you want to die. This man is dead, she thought, all those beings doomed to die are already dead, all it takes is for me to flick them lightly with my thumb or to send them a violet-coloured letter that they cannot refuse. This man isn't dead, she thought, in a few hours' time he'll wake up, he'll get out of bed as he does every day, he'll open the back door to let the dog out into the garden to relieve itself, he'll eat his breakfast, he'll go into the bath-room from where he'll emerge refreshed, washed and shaved, perhaps he'll sally forth into the street, taking the dog with him so that they can buy the morning newspaper together at the corner kiosk, perhaps he'll sit down in front of the music stand and again play the three pieces by schumann, perhaps afterwards he'll think about death as all human beings must, although he's unaware that at this very moment, he is as if immortal, because the figure of death looking at him doesn't know how to kill him. The man changed position, turned his back on the wardrobe blocking the door and let his right arm slide down towards the side on which the dog is lying. A minute later, he was awake. He was thirsty. He turned on his bedside light, got up, shuffled his feet into the slippers which were, as always, providing a pillow for the dog's head, and went into the kitchen. Death followed him. The man filled a glass with water and drank it. At this point, the dog appeared, slaked his thirst in the water-dish next to the back door and then looked up at his master. I suppose you want to go out, said the cellist. He opened the door and waited until the animal came back. A little water remained in his glass. Death looked at it and made an effort to imagine what it must be like to feel thirsty, but failed. She would have been equally incapable of imag-ining it when she'd had to make people die of thirst in the desert, but at the time she hadn't even tried. The dog returned, wagging his tail. Let's go back to sleep, said the man. They went into the bedroom again, the dog turned round twice, then curled up into a ball. The man drew the sheet up to his neck, coughed twice and soon afterwards was asleep again. Sitting in her corner, death was watching. Much later, the dog got up from the carpet and jumped onto the sofa. For the first time in her life, death knew what it felt like to have a dog on her lap.

WE'VE ALL HAD OUR MOMENTS OF WEAKNESS, AND IF WE MANAGE to get through today without any, we'll be sure to have some tomorrow. Just as beneath the bronze cuirass of achilles there once beat a sentimental heart, think only of the hero's ten years of jealousy after agamemnon stole away his beloved, the slave-girl briseis, and then the terrible rage that made him return to war, howling out his wrath at the trojans when his friend patro-clus was killed by hector, so, beneath the most impenetrable of armours ever forged and guaranteed to remain impenetrable until the end of time, we are referring here, of course, to death's skeleton, there is always a chance that one day something will casually insinuate itself into the dread carcass, a soft chord from a cello, an ingenuous trill on a piano, or the mere sight of some sheet music open on a chair, which will make you remember the thing you refuse to think about, that you have never lived and that, do what you may, you never will live, unless . . . You had sat coolly observing the sleeping cellist, that man whom you could not kill because you got to him when it was too late, you saw the dog curled up on the carpet, and you were unable to touch that creature either, because you are not his death, and in the warm darkness of the room, those two living beings who, having surrendered to sleep, didn't even know you were there, only served to fill your consciousness with an awareness of the depth of your failure. In that apartment, you, who had grown used to being able to do what no one else can, saw how impo-tent you were, tied hand and foot, with your double-o-seven

144

licence to kill rendered null and void, never, admit it, not in all your days as death, had you felt so humiliated. It was then that you left the bedroom for the music room, where you knelt down before suite number six for the cello by johann sebastian bach and made those rapid movements with your shoulders which, in human beings, usually accompany convulsive sobbing, it was then, with your hard knees digging into the hard floor, that your exasperation suddenly vanished like the imponderable mist into which you sometimes transform yourself when you don't wish to be entirely invisible. You returned to the bedroom, you followed the cellist when he went into the kitchen to get a drink of water and open the back door for the dog, first, you'd seen him lying down asleep, now you saw him awake and standing up, and perhaps due to the optical illusion caused by the vertical stripes on his pyjamas he seemed much taller than you, but that was impossible, it was just a trick of the eyes, a distortion due to perspective, the pure logic of facts tells us that you, death, are the biggest, bigger than everything else, bigger than all of us. Or perhaps you're not always the biggest, perhaps the things that happen in the world can be explained by chance, for example, the dazzling moonlight that the musician remembers from his childhood would have shone in vain if he had been asleep, yes, chance, because you were once again a very small death when you returned to the bedroom and went and sat down on the sofa, and smaller still when the dog got up from the carpet and jumped onto your girlish lap, and then you had such a lovely thought, you thought how unfair it was that death, not you, the other death, would one day come and douse the mild embers of that soft animal warmth, that is what you thought, imagine that, you who are so accustomed to the arctic and antarctic cold of the room to which you have returned and to which the voice of your ominous duty summoned you, the duty to kill the man who, as he slept, seemed to bear on his face the bitter rictus of one who has never shared his bed with a truly human companion, who had an agreement with this dog that they would each dream about the other, the dog about the man, the man about the dog, this man who gets up in the night in his striped pyjamas to go to the kitchen for a drink of water, obviously it would be easier to take a glass of water to his room when he goes to bed, but he doesn't do that, he prefers his little night-time saunter down the corridor to the kitchen, in the midst of the peace and silence of the night, with the dog who always follows him and sometimes asks to be let out in the garden, but not always, This man must die, you say.

Death is once again a skeleton swathed in a shroud, with the hood low over her forehead, so that the worst of her skull remains covered, although it was hardly worth going to the trouble of covering up, if this really did concern her, because there's no one here to be frightened by the macabre spectacle, and especially since all that can be seen are the tips of the bones of fingers and toes, the latter resting on the flagstones, whose icy chill they do not feel, the former leafing, like a rasp, through the pages of the complete volume of death's historic ordinances, from the first of all rules, which was set down in three simple words, thou shalt kill, to the more recent addenda and appendices, in which all the manners and variants of dying so far known are listed, and you could say of that list that it was inexhaustible. Death was not surprised by the negative results of her researches, it would, in fact, be incongruous, more than that, superfluous, to find in a book that determines for each and every representative of the human race a full stop, a conclusion, an end, a death, such words as life and live, such words as I'm alive and I will live. There is only room in that book for death, not for absurd hypotheses about what to do if someone escapes death. That has never been known. Perhaps, if you looked hard, you might find once, and only once, in some unnecessary foot-note, the words I lived, but that search was never seriously attempted, which leads one to conclude that there is a very good reason why not even the fact of having lived deserves a mention in the book of death. And the reason is that the other name for the book of death, as it behoves us to know, is the book of noth-ingness. The skeleton pushed the regulations to one side and stood up. As was her custom when she needed to get to the nub of a problem, she walked twice round the room, then she opened the drawer in the filing cabinet that contained the cellist's card and took it out. Her gesture has just reminded us that now is the moment, now or never, yet another instance of chance, to clarify an important aspect relating to the functioning of these archives and about which, due to reprehensible neglect on the part of the narrator, we have not yet spoken. Firstly, and contrary to what you may have imagined, the ten million index cards filed away in these drawers were not filled out by death, they were not written by her. Certainly not, death is death, not a common clerk. The cards appear in their places, arranged alpha-betically, at the exact moment when someone is born, only to disappear at the exact moment when that person dies. Before the invention of the violet-coloured letters, death didn't even go to the trouble of opening the drawers, the comings and goings of the cards took place without any fuss or confusion, there is no memory of there ever having been any embarrassing scenes with some people saying they didn't want to be born and others protesting that they didn't want to die. The cards of the people who die go, without anyone having to take them, to a room below this one, or, rather, they take their place in one of the rooms that lie in layer upon subterranean layer, going ever deeper, and which are already well on the way to the fiery centre of the earth, where all this paperwork will one day burn. Here, in the room occupied by death and the scythe, it would be impossible to establish a similar criterion to the one adopted by a certain registrar who decided to bring together in one archive the names and documents belonging to the living and the dead under his protection, yes, every single one, alleging that only when they were brought together could they represent humanity as it should be understood, an absolute whole, independent of time and place, and that keeping them separate until then had been an attack upon the spirit. That is the enormous difference between the death we see before us now and the sensible registrar with his papers of life and death, while she prides herself on her olympian disdain for those who have died, we should remember the cruel phrase, so often repeated, which says that what's past is past, he, on the other hand, thanks to what we, in current phraseology, call historical awareness, believes that the living should never be separated from the dead and that, if they are, not only will the dead remain for ever dead, the living will only half-live their lives, even if they turn out to live as long as methuselah, about whom, by the way, there is some dispute as to whether he died at nine hundred and sixty-nine as stated in the ancient masoretic text or at seven hundred and twenty as stated in the samaritan pentateuch. Clearly not everyone will be in agreement with the daring archivistic plan put forward by that registrar of all the names given and yet to be given, but we will leave it here, in case it should prove useful in the future.

Death examines the card and finds nothing on it that she has not seen before, that is, the biography of a musician who should have died a week ago and who, nevertheless, continues to live quietly in his modest artist's home, with his black dog who climbs onto ladies' laps, with his piano and his cello, his nocturnal bouts of thirst and his striped pyjamas. There must be a way of resolving this dilemma, thought death, it would be preferable, of course, if the matter could be sorted out without drawing too much attention to it, but if the highest authorities serve any purpose, if they are not there merely to have honours and praise heaped upon them, then they now have an excellent opportunity to show that they are not indifferent to those down here labouring away on the plains, let them change the regulations, let them impose some special measures, let them authorise, if it comes to that, some act of dubious legality, anything but allow such a scandal to continue. The curious thing about this case is that death has no idea who they actually are, these high authorities who should, in theory, resolve this dilemma. It's true that in one of the letters she had written and which was published in the press, the second one if we're not mistaken, she had referred to a universal death who would, although no one knew when, do away with all manifestations of life in the universe down to the last microbe, but this, as well as being a philosophical commonplace, since nothing, not even death, can last for ever, originated, in practical terms, from a common-sense deduction that had long been doing the rounds of the various deaths in their different sectors, although it remained to be confirmed by a knowledge backed up by study and experience. It's us sectorial deaths, thought death, who do the real work of removing any excrescences, and it wouldn't surprise me in the least if, should the cosmos ever disappear, it won't be as a consequence of some solemn proclamation by that universal death, echoing around the galaxies and the black holes, but merely the accumulation of all those little private and personal deaths that are our responsibility, one by one, as if the proverbial chicken, instead of filling its crop grain by grain, grain by grain, began foolishly to empty it out, because that, I reckon, is what is most likely to happen with life, which is busily preparing its own end, with no need of any help from us, not even waiting for us to give it a helping hand. Death's perplexity is perfectly understandable. She was placed in this world so long ago that she can no longer remember from whom she received the necessary instructions to carry out the job she was charged with. They placed the regulations in her hands, pointed out the words thou shalt kill as the one guiding light of her future activities and told her, doubtless not noticing the macabre irony, to get on with her life. And she did, thinking that, in case of doubt or some unlikely mistake, she would always have her back covered, there would always be someone, a boss, a superior, a spiritual guru, of whom she could ask advice and guidance.

It's hard to believe, therefore, and here we enter at last into the cold, objective analysis for which the situation of death and the cellist has long been crying out, that an information system as perfect as the one that has kept these archives updated over millennia, continually revising the data, making index cards appear and disappear as people were born or died, it's hard to believe, we repeat, that such a system should be so primitive and so unidirectional that the information source, wherever it is, isn't, in turn, constantly receiving all the data resulting from the daily activities of death on the ground, so to speak. And if it does receive that data and fails to react to the extraordinary news that someone didn't die when they should have, then one of two things is happening, either, against all our logic and natural expectations, it finds the episode of no interest and therefore feels no obligation to inter- vene in order to neutralise any difficulties caused, or we must assume that death, contrary to what she herself believes, has carte blanche to resolve, as she sees fit, any problem that may arise during her day-to-day work. The word doubt had to be spoken once or twice here before it rang a bell in death's memory, for there was a passage in the regulations which, because it was written in very small print and appeared only as a footnote, neither attracted nor fixed the attention of the studious. Putting down the cellist's index card, death picked up the book. She knew that what she was looking for would be neither in the appendices nor in the addenda, that it must be in the early part of the regulations, the oldest and therefore the least often consulted part, as tends to be the case with basic historical texts, and there she found it. This is what it said, In case of doubt, death must, as quickly as possible, take whatever measures her experience tells her to take in order to fulfil the desideratum that should at all times guide her actions, that is, to put an end to human lives when the time prescribed for them at birth has expired, even if to achieve that effect she has to resort to less orthodox methods in situations where the person puts up an abnormal degree of resistance to the fatal judgement or where there are anomalous factors that could not have been foreseen at the time these regulations were drawn up. It couldn't be clearer, death has a free hand to act as she thinks best. This, as our examination of the matter will show, was hardly a novelty. Just look at the facts. When death, on her own account and at her own risk, decided to suspend her activities from the first day of january this year, the idea didn't even enter her empty head that some superior in the hierarchy might ask her to justify her bizarre behaviour, just as she didn't even consider the high probability that her picturesque invention of the violet-coloured letters would be frowned on by that same superior or by another even higher up. These are the dangerous consequences of working on automatic pilot, of stultifying routine, of doing the same job for too long. A person, or death, it really doesn't matter, scrupulously fulfills her duties, day after day, encountering no problems, no doubts, concentrating entirely on following the rules established by those above, and if, after a time, no one comes noseying around into how she carries out her work, then one thing is sure, that person, and this is what happened with death, will end up behaving, without her realising it, as if she were queen and mistress of all that she does, and not only that, but of when and how she should do it too. That is the only reasonable explanation for why it never occurred to death to ask her superiors for authorisation when she made and implemented the important decisions we have described and without which this story, for good or ill, could not exist. She didn't even think to do so. And now, paradoxically, precisely at the moment when she cannot contain her joy at discovering that the power to dispose of human lives as she sees fit is, after all, hers alone and that she will not be called upon to explain herself to anyone, not today or ever, just when the scent of glory is threatening to befuddle her senses, she cannot suppress the kind of fearful thought that might assail someone who, just as they were about to be found out, miraculously, at the very last moment, escaped exposure, Phew, that was a close shave.

Nevertheless, the death who now rises from her chair is an empress. She shouldn't be living in this freezing subterranean room, as if she had been buried alive, but on top of the highest mountain presiding over the fates of the world, gazing benevolently down on the human herd, watching them as they rush hither and thither, unaware that they're heading in the same direction, that one step forward will take them just as close to death as one step back, that it makes no difference because everything will have but one ending, the ending that a part of yourself will always have to think about and which is the black stain on your hopeless humanity. Death is holding the index card in her hand. She is conscious that she must do something with it, but she doesn't know quite what. First, she must calm down and remember that she is the same death she was before, nothing more, nothing less, that the only difference between today and yesterday is that she is more certain of who she is. Second, the fact that she can finally have it out with the cellist is no reason to forget to send today's letters. She had only to think this and instantly two hundred and eighty-four index cards appeared on the desk, half were of men and half of women, and with them two hundred and eighty-four sheets of paper and two hundred and eighty-four envelopes. Death sat down again, put the index card to one side and began to write. The very last grain of sand in a four-hour hourglass would have just slipped through as she finished signing the two hundred and eightieth letter. An hour later, the envelopes were sealed and ready to be despatched. Death went to fetch the letter that had been sent three times and returned three times and placed it on the pile of violet-coloured envelopes, I'm going to give you one last chance, she said. She made the customary gesture with her left hand and the letters disappeared. Not even ten seconds had passed before the letter to the musician silently reappeared on the desk. Then death said, If that's how you want it, fine. She crossed out the date of birth on the index card and changed it to the following year, then she amended his age, and where fifty was written, she changed it to forty-nine. You can't do that, said the scythe, It's done, There'll be consequences, Only one, What's that, The death, at last, of that wretched cellist who's been having a laugh at my expense, But the poor man doesn't know he should be dead, As far as I'm concerned, he might as well know it, Even so, you don't have the power or the authority to change an index card, That's where you're wrong, I have all the power and authority I need, I'm death, and never more so than from this day forward, You don't know what you're getting into, warned the scythe, There's only one place in the world that death can't get into, Where's that, What they call a coffin, casket, tomb, funeral urn, vault, sepulchre, I can't enter there, only the living can, once I've killed them, of course, All those words to say the same sad thing, That's what these people are like, they're never quite sure what they mean.

DEATH HAS A PLAN. CHANGING THE MUSICIAN'S YEAR OF BIRTH was only the opening move in an operation which, we can tell you now, will deploy some quite exceptional methods never before used in the history of the relationship between the human race and its oldest, most mortal enemy. As in a game of chess, death advanced her queen. A few more moves should open the way to a checkmate, and the game will end. One might now ask why death doesn't simply revert to the statu quo ante, when people died simply because they had to, with no waiting around for the postman to bring them a violet-coloured letter. The question has its logic, but the reply is no less logical. It is, firstly, a matter of honour, determination and professional pride, for if death were to return to the innocence of former times, it would, in the eyes of everyone, be tanta-mount to admitting defeat. Since the current process involves the use of violet-coloured letters, then these must be the means by which the cellist will die. We need only put ourselves in death's place to understand the rationale behind this. As we have seen on four previous occasions, there remains the prin-cipal problem of delivering that now weary letter to its addressee, and if the longed-for goal is to be achieved, that is where the exceptional methods we referred to above come in. But let us not anticipate events, let us see what death is doing now. At this precise moment, death is not actually doing anything more than she usually does, she is, to use a current expression, hanging loose, although, to tell the truth, it would

154

be more exact to say that death never hangs loose, death simply is. At the same time and everywhere. She doesn't need to run after people to catch them, she will always be where they are. Now, thanks to this new method of warning people by letter, she could, if she chose to, just sit quietly in her subterranean room and wait for the mail to do the work, but she is, by nature, strong, energetic and active. As the old saying goes, You can't cage a barnyard chicken. In the figurative sense, death is a barnyard chicken. She won't be so stupid, or so unforgivably weak, as to repress what is best in her, her limitlessly expansive nature, therefore she will not repeat the painful process of concentrating all her energies on remaining at the very edge of visibility without actually going over to the other side, as she did the previous night, and at what a cost, during the hours she spent in the musician's apartment. Since, as we have said a thousand and one times, she is present everywhere, she is there too. The dog is sleeping in the garden, in the sun, waiting for his master to come home. He doesn't know where his master has gone or what he has gone to do, and the idea of following his trail, were he ever to try, is something he has ceased to think about, for the good and bad smells in a capital city are so many and so disorienting. We never consider that the things dogs know about us are things of which we have not the faintest notion. Death, however, knows that the cellist is sitting on the stage of a theatre, to the right of the conductor, in the place that corresponds to the instrument he plays, she sees him moving the bow with his skilful right hand, she sees his no less skilful left hand moving up and down the strings, just as she herself had done in the half-dark, even though she has never learned music, not even the basics of music theory, so-called three-four time. The conductor stopped the rehearsal, tapping his baton on the edge of the music stand to make some comment and to issue an order, in this passage, he wants the cellists, and only the cellists, to make themselves heard, while, at the same time, appearing not to be making a sound, a kind of musical charade which the musicians appear to have mastered without difficulty, that is what art is like, things that seem impossible to the layperson turn out not to be. Death, needless to say, fills the whole theatre, right to the very top, as far as the allegorical paintings on the ceiling and the vast unlit chandelier, but the view she prefers at the moment is the view from a box just above the stage, very close, and slightly at an angle to the section of strings that play the lower notes, the violas, the contraltos of the violin family, the cellos, which are the equivalent of the bass, and the double-basses, which have the deepest voice of all. Death is sitting there, on a narrow crimson-upholstered chair, and staring fixedly at the first cellist, the one she watched while he was asleep and who wears striped pyjamas, the one who owns a dog that is, at this moment, sleeping in the sun in the garden, waiting for his master to return. That is her man, a musician, nothing more, like the almost one hundred other men and women seated in a semicircle around their personal shaman, the conductor, and all of whom will, one day, in some future week or month or year, receive a violet-coloured letter and leave their place empty, until some other violinist, flautist or trumpeter comes to sit in the same chair, perhaps with another shaman waving a baton to conjure forth sounds, life is an orchestra which is always playing, in tune or out, a titanic that is always sinking and always rising to the surface, and it is then that it occurs to death that she would be left with nothing to do if the sunken ship never managed to rise again, singing the evocative song sung by the waters as they cascade from her decks, like the watery song, dripping like a murmurous sigh over her undulating body, sung by the goddess amphitrite at her birth, when she became she who circles the seas, for that is the meaning of the name she was given. Death wonders where amphitrite is now, the daughter of nereus and doris, where is she now, she who may never have existed in reality, but who nevertheless briefly inhabited the human mind in order to create in it, again only briefly, a certain way of giving meaning to the world, of finding ways of understanding reality. But they didn't understand it, thought death, nor will they, however hard they try, because everything in their lives is provisional, precarious, transitory, gods, men, the past, all gone, what is will not always be, and even I, death, will come to an end when there's no one left to kill, either in the traditional manner, or by correspondence. We know that this is not the first time such a thought has passed through whatever part of her it is that thinks, but it was the first time that thinking it had brought her such a feeling of profound relief, like that of someone who, having completed a task, slowly leans back to take a rest. Suddenly the orchestra fell silent, all that can be heard is the sound of a cello, it's what they call a solo, a modest solo that will last, at most, two minutes, it's as if from the forces invoked by the shaman a voice had arisen, speaking perhaps in the name of all those who are now silent, even the conductor doesn't move, he's looking at the same musician who left open on a chair the sheet music of suite number six opus one thousand and twelve in d major by johann sebastian bach, a suite he will never play in this theatre, because he is merely a cellist in the orchestra, albeit the leader of his section, not one of those famous concert artistes who travel the world playing and giving interviews, receiving flowers, applause, plaudits and medals, he's lucky that he occasionally gets a few bars to play solo, thanks to some generous composer who happened to remember the side of the orchestra where little of anything out of the ordinary tends to happen. When the rehearsal ends, he'll put his cello in its case and take a taxi home, a taxi with a large boot, and maybe tonight, after supper, he'll put the sheet music for the bach suite on the stand, take a deep breath and draw the bow across the strings so that the first note thus born can console him for the irredeemable banalities of the world and so that the second, if possible, will make him forget them, the solo ends, the rest of the orchestra covers the last echo of the cello, and the shaman, with an imperious wave of his baton, has returned to his role as invoker and guide of the spirits of sound. Death is proud of how well her cellist played. As if she were a family member, his mother, his sister, his fiancée, not his wife, though, because this man has never married.

Over the next three days, apart from the time it took her to run to the subterranean room, hurriedly write the letters and send them off, death was more than his shadow, she was the very air he breathed. Shadows have a grave defect, they lose their place, they vanish the moment there's no source of light. Death travelled next to him in the taxi that took him home, she went into his apartment when he did, she observed benevolently the dog's wild effusions at the arrival of his master, and then, like someone invited to spend a little time there, she made herself comfortable. It's easy enough for someone who doesn't need to move, she doesn't mind whether she's sitting on the floor or perched on top of a wardrobe. The orchestra rehearsal had finished late, it will soon be dark. The cellist gave the dog some food, then prepared his own supper from the contents of two cans, heated up whatever needed heating up, put a cloth on the kitchen table, along with knife, fork and napkin, poured some wine into a glass and, unhurriedly, as if he were thinking about something else, put the first forkful of food in his mouth. The dog sat down beside him, any leftovers that his master might leave on his plate and proffer to him on his hand will serve as his dessert. Death looks at the cellist.

She can't really tell the difference between ugly people and pretty people, because, since she is familiar only with her own skull, she has an irresistible tendency to imagine the outline of the skull beneath the face that serves as our shop window. Basically, if truth be told, in death's eyes we are all equally ugly, even in the days when we might have been beauty queens or their male equivalent. She admires the cellist's strong fingers, she guesses that the tips of the fingers on his left hand must have gradually grown harder, perhaps even slightly calloused, life can be unfair in this and other ways, the left hand is a case in point, for even though it does all the hard work on the cello, it receives far less applause from the audience than the right hand. Once supper was over, the cellist washed the dishes, carefully folded the table cloth and the napkin, put them in a drawer in the cupboard and, before leaving the kitchen, looked around to see if anything was out of place. The dog followed him into the music room, where death was waiting for them. Contrary to the supposition we made while in the theatre, the cellist did not play the bach suite. One day, in conversation with some colleagues in the orchestra who were talking jokingly about the possibility of composing musical portraits, genuine ones, not just pictures of types, like mussorgsky's portraits of samuel goldenberg and schmuyle, he said that, assuming such a thing really were possible in music, they would find his portrait not in any cello composition, but in the briefest of chopin études, opus twenty-five, number nine, in g flat major. When asked why, he replied that he simply couldn't see himself in any other piece of music and that this seemed to him the best of reasons. And that in the space of fifty-eight seconds chopin had said all there was to say about someone he could never possibly have met. For a few days, by way of an amiable joke, the wittier orchestra members called him fifty-eight seconds, but the nickname was far too long to stick, and, besides, it's impossible to keep up a dialogue with someone who has decided to take fifty-eight seconds to reply to any question put to him. In the end, the cellist won this friendly contest. As if he had sensed the presence in his house of a third person, to whom, for unexplained reasons, he felt he should talk about himself, and wishing to avoid having to make the long speech which even the simplest of lives requires in order to say anything of substance, the cellist sat down at the piano, and after a brief pause for the audience to settle, he launched into the piece. Lying half asleep next to the music stand, the dog didn't appear to give much importance to the storm of sound unleashed above his head, perhaps because he had heard it before, perhaps because it added nothing to what he already knew about his master. Death, however, who, in the line of duty, had listened to a great deal of music, notably that same composer chopin's funeral march and the adagio assai from beethoven's third symphony, she, for the first time in her very long life, had a sense of what might well be the perfect blend of what is said and the way in which it is said. She didn't much care if it was or wasn't the musical portrait of the cellist, it's likely that he'd fabricated in his mind any alleged similarities, real or imagined, but what impressed death was that she seemed to hear in those fifty-eight seconds of music a rhythmical and melodic transposition of every and any human life, be it run-of-the-mill or extraordinary, because of its tragic brevity, its desperate intensity, and also because of that final chord, like an ellipsis left hanging in the air, something yet to be said. The cellist had fallen into one of the least forgivable of human sins, that of presumption, when he thought he could see his face, and his alone, in a portrait in which everyone could be found, a presumption which, however, if we think about it, if we choose not to remain on the surface of things, could equally be interpreted as a manifestation of its polar opposite, that is, of humility, since if it is a portrait of everyone, then I must be included in it too. Death hesitates, she can't quite decide between presumption and humility, and to break the deadlock, to decide once and for all, she amuses herself now by observing the cellist, waiting for the expression on his face to reveal to her what she needs to know, or perhaps his hands, for the hands are like two open books, not for the real or supposed reasons put forward by chiromancy, with its heart lines and its life lines, yes, life, ladies and gentlemen, you heard correctly, life, but because they speak when they open and close, when they caress or strike, when they wipe away a tear or disguise a smile, when they rest on a shoulder or wave goodbye, when they work, when they are still, when they sleep, when they wake, and then death, having finished her observations, concluded that it isn't true that the antonym of presumption is humility, even if all the dictionaries in the world swear blind that it is, poor dictionaries, who have to rule themselves and us only with the words that exist, when there are so many words still missing, for example, this word that should be the polar opposite of presumption, but never the bowed head of humility, the word that we see clearly written on the face and hands of the cellist, but which cannot tell us what it is called.

The next day, it so happened, was a Sunday. When the weather is fine, as it is today, the cellist is in the habit of spending the morning in one of the city parks with his dog and a book or two. The dog never wanders far, even when instinct makes him move from tree to tree sniffing his fellow canines' pee. He lifts his leg now and then, but goes no further in the satisfaction of his excretory needs. The other, shall we say, complementary procedure, he conscientiously carries out in the garden of the house where he lives, so that the cellist doesn't have to chase after him to pick up his excrement and deposit it in a plastic bag with the help of a little spade specially designed for the purpose. This might have been merely a notable example of good canine training were it not for the extraordinary fact that the idea came from the dog, who is of the opinion that a musician, a cellist, an artist who struggles to be able to give a decent rendition of suite number six opus one thousand and twelve in d major by bach did not come into this world in order to pick up the still-steaming poop of his dog or anyone else's. It simply isn't right. As he said one day during a conversation with his master, bach never had to do that. The musician replied that times had changed a lot since then, but had to admit that bach would certainly never have had to do that. Although the musician is clearly a lover of literature in general, a look at an average shelf in his library will show that he has a special liking for books on astronomy, the natural sciences and nature, and today he has brought with him a handbook on entomology. He doesn't have any background knowledge, and so he doesn't expect to glean very much from it, but he enjoys learning that there are nearly a million species of insect on earth and that these are divided into two orders, the pterygotes, which have wings, and the apterygotes, which do not, and that they are in turn classified as orthopterus, like the grasshopper, or blattodea, like the cockroach, mantodea, like the praying mantis, neuroptera, like the chrysopa, odonata, like the dragonfly, ephemeroptera, like the mayfly, trichoptera, like the caddis fly, isoptera, like the termite, aphaniptera, like the flea, anoplura, like the louse, mallophaga, like the bird louse, heteroptera, like the bedbug, homoptera, like the plant louse, diptera, like the fly, hymenoptera, like the wasp, lepidoptera, like the death's head moth, coleoptera, like the beetle, and finally, thysanura, like the silver fish. As you can see from the image in the book, the death's head moth, a nocturnal moth, whose latin name is acherontia atropos, bears on the back of its thorax a pattern resembling a human skull, it reaches a wingspan of twelve centimetres and is dark in colour, its lower wings being yellow and black. And we call it atropos, that is, death. The musician doesn't know it, nor could he ever even have imagined such a possibility, but death is gazing, fascinated, over his shoulder, at the colour photograph of the moth. Fascinated, and confused too. Remember that another of the parcae, not this one, is in charge of the insects' passage from life to non-life, that is to say, of killing them, and although in many cases the modus operandi may be the same for both, the exceptions are numerous too, suffice it to say that insects do not die from such common human diseases as, for example, pneumonia, tuberculosis, cancer, acquired immuno-deficiency syndrome, more commonly known as aids, from car crashes or cardiovascular diseases. This much anyone can understand. What is harder to grasp, and what is confusing death as she continues to peer over the cellist's shoulder, is that a human skull, drawn with such extraordinary precision, should have appeared, who knows in which period of creation, on the hairy back of a moth. Of course, little moths and butter-flies have been known to appear on the human body too, but they have never been anything more than a primitive artifice, mere tattoos, they were not with the person from birth. There was probably a time, thinks death, when all living beings were one, but then, gradually, with increasing specialisation, they found themselves divided up into five kingdoms, namely, monera, protista, fungi, plants and animals, within which, within those kingdoms that is, infinite macrospecialisations and microspecialisations occurred over the ages, although it is hardly surprising that, in the midst of all this confusion, this biological mêlée, the particularities of some would be repeated in others. This would explain, for example, the disquieting presence of a white skull on the back of this moth, acherontia atropos, whose name, curiously enough, contains not only another word for death, but also the name of one of the rivers that flows through hades, it would also explain the equally disquieting similarities between the mandrake root and the human body. It's hard to know what to think when confronted by all these marvels of nature, by such sublime surprises. However, the thoughts preoccupying death, who continues to stare over the cellist's shoulder, have already taken another route. Now she is feeling sad because she is comparing how it would have been had she used death's head moths as messengers rather than those stupid violet-coloured letters, which, at the time, had seemed to her such a brilliant idea. It would never occur to one of those moths to turn back, it carries its duty emblazoned on its thorax, that was what it was born for. Besides, the effect as spectacle would be totally different, instead of a common-or-garden postman handing us a letter, we would see twelve centimetres of moth hovering above our head, the angel of darkness showing off its black and yellow wings, and suddenly, after skimming the earth and tracing a circle around us from which we would never step free, it would rise vertically and place its skull in front of ours. We would, of course, be unstinting in our applause for their acrobatics. One can see that the death in charge of us human beings still has a lot to learn. As we well know, moths do not come under her jurisdiction. Neither they, nor any of the other, almost infinite animal species. She would have to reach an agreement with her colleague in the zoological department, the one with responsibility for these natural products, and ask to borrow a few acherontia atropos, although, regrettably, bearing in mind the vast difference in scope of their respective territories and of their corresponding populations, it is more than likely that the aforementioned colleague would reply with a proud, brusque and peremptory no, because lack of solidarity is no mere empty expression, even in the realm of death. Think only of the million species of insect cited in that basic entomology book, imagine, if you can, the number of individuals in each species, and do you not think that there must be more tiny creatures on this earth than there are stars in the sky, or in sidereal space, if you prefer to give a poetic name to the convulsive reality of the universe in which we are nothing but a tiny scrap of shit on the point of dissolving. The death in charge of the human race, who currently comprise a mere bagatelle of seven billion men and women rather unevenly distributed over the five continents, is a secondary, subaltern death, she herself is perfectly aware of her place in the hierarchy of thanatos, as she was honest enough to acknowledge in the letter she sent to the newspaper that had printed her name with a capital d. Meanwhile, given that the door of dreams is so easy to push open, and that dreams are so freely available to everyone that we don't even have to pay tax on them, death, who has now ceased peering over the cellist's shoulder, enjoys herself imagining what it would be like to have at her command a battalion of moths all lined up on the desk, with her doing the roll call and giving the orders, go there, find such-and-such a person, show them the death's head on your back and return. The musician would think that his acherontia atropos had flown up from the open page, that would be his last thought and the last image he would take with him fixed on his retina, not some fat woman dressed in black announcing his death, like the one seen, so they say, by marcel proust, or an ogre wrapped in a white sheet, as the more perspicacious claim to have seen from their deathbed. A moth, just a rustle of silk wings from a large, dark moth with, on its back, a white mark shaped like a skull.

The cellist looked at the clock and saw that it was long past lunchtime. The dog, who had been thinking exactly this for some ten minutes, had sat down beside his owner and, with his head resting on his master's knee, was waiting patiently for him to return to the world. Nearby was a small restaurant providing sandwiches and other such culinary trifles. On the mornings that he visited the park, the cellist was a regular customer there, and he always ordered the same thing. Two tuna mayo sandwiches and a glass of wine for him, and a beef sandwich, rare, for the dog. If the weather was fine, as today, they sat on the grass, in the shade of a tree, and while they were eating, they talked. The dog always kept the best until last, he began by dispatching the slices of bread and only then did he give himself over to the pleasures of the meat, chewing unhurriedly, conscientiously, savouring the juices. The cellist ate distractedly, without giving any thought to what he was eating, he was pondering that suite in d major by bach, in particular the prelude and one fiendishly difficult passage that would sometimes make him pause, hesitate, doubt, which is the worst thing that can happen in the life of a musician. After they had eaten, they lay down side by side, the cellist dozed a little, and, a minute later, the dog was asleep. When they woke and went home, death went with them. While the dog ran into the garden to empty its bowels, the cellist placed the music for the bach suite on the stand, found the tricky bit, a truly diabolical pianissimo, and again experienced that implacable moment of hesitation. Death felt sorry for him, Poor thing, and the worst of it is that he's not going to have time to get it right, not, of course, that anyone ever does, even those who come close are always wide of the mark. Then, for the first time, death noticed that nowhere in the apartment was there a single photograph of a woman, apart from that of an elderly lady who was clearly the cellist's mother, accompanied by a man who must have been his father.

I HAVE A BIG FAVOUR TO ASK OF YOU, SAID DEATH. AS USUAL, the scythe did not respond, the only sign that it had heard was a barely perceptible shudder, a generalised expression of physical dismay, for such words, asking a favour, and a big favour to boot, had never emerged from death's mouth before. I'm going to be away for a week, death went on, and during that time, I need you to take over from me as regards despatching the letters, obviously I'm not asking you to write them, you only have to send them, all you've got to do is give out a kind of mental command and create an inner vibration in your blade, a feeling, an emotion, anything to show you're alive, that will be enough to ensure that the letters set off for their destination. The scythe remained silent, but that silence was the equivalent of a question. It's just that I can't keep coming and going to deal with the post, said death, I must concentrate entirely on solving this problem with the cellist and finding a way of giving him that wretched letter. The scythe was waiting. Death went on, This is what I plan to do, I'll write all the letters for the week I'll be away, something which, given the exceptional nature of the situation, I can allow myself to do, and, as I said, you only have to send them, you won't even have to move from that spot, leaning against the wall, and I'm being very nice about it, you know, I'm asking you to do this as a favour to me as a friend, when, of course, I could dispense with the niceties and simply issue an order, because the fact that I haven't made much use of you in recent years doesn't mean that you're not still at my service. The scythe's resigned silence confirmed that this was true. So we agree then, concluded death, I'll spend the rest of the day writing letters, there should, I reckon, be about two thousand and fifty, imagine that, it'll mean working my fingers to the bone, I'll leave them for you on the desk, in separate groups, from left to right, don't forget, from left to right, got that, from here to here, I'll be in another fine mess if people start receiving their notifications at the wrong time, either early or late. They say that silence gives consent. The scythe remained silent, and therefore gave its consent. Wrapped in her sheet, with the hood thrown back so as not to hamper her vision, death sat down to work. She wrote and wrote, the hours passed and still she wrote, there were the letters, there were the envelopes, and then she had to fold the letters and seal the envelopes, some will ask how she could manage this if she has no tongue nor any source of saliva, that, my friends, was in the good old days of make do and mend, when we were still living in the stone age of a modernity that had barely begun to dawn, nowadays envelopes are self-seal, just peel off the little strip of paper and bob's your uncle, in fact, you might say that of all the many uses to which the tongue has been put, this one is now a thing of the past. Death did indeed work her fingers to the bone, because, of course, she is all bone. This is typical of phrases that become fixed in language, and which we continue to use long after they've deviated from their original sense, forgetting that death, for example, who is, of course, a skeleton, is nothing but bone anyway, you need only look at an X-ray. The usual dismissive gesture sent today's two hundred and eighty or so envelopes off into hyperspace, which means that only from tomorrow will the scythe take up the functions of official sender with which it has just been entrusted. Without a word, without so much as a goodbye or a see you later, death got up from her chair, went over to the only door in the room, that narrow little door to which we have often referred, although we haven't the slightest idea where it might lead, opened it, passed through and closed it after her. The thrill of this made the scythe tremble from the very tip of its blade to the base. Never in the scythe's memory had that door been used.

The hours passed, the hours necessary for the sun to come up outside, not here in this cold, white room, where the pale bulbs, which are always lit, seem to have been placed to fend off the shadows from a corpse who is afraid of the dark. It is still too early for the scythe to give the order that will make the second pile of letters vanish from the room, and so it can sleep a little more. This is what insomniacs say when they have not slept a wink all night, thinking, poor things, that they can fool sleep by asking for a little more, just a little more, when they have not yet been granted one minute of repose. Alone for all those hours, the scythe tried to find an explanation for the remarkable fact that death had made her exit through a sealed door, one that had been eternally condemned, certainly for as long as the scythe has been here. In the end, it gave up any attempt to understand, sooner or later, it will find out what's going on behind that door, for it's almost impossible for there to be secrets between death and the scythe, just as there are no secrets between the sickle and the hand that wields it. The scythe did not have to wait long. Only half an hour of clock time could have passed when the door opened and a woman appeared. The scythe had heard that such a thing was possible, that death could transform herself into a human being, preferably female, this being her normal gender, but had always thought it a mere tale, a myth, a legend like so many others, for example, the phoenix reborn from its own ashes, the man in the moon carrying a bundle of firewood on his back because he had worked on the sabbath, baron munchausen saving himself and his horse from drowning in a swamp by pulling on his own hair, the dracula of transylvania who cannot die, however many times he is killed, unless a stake is driven through his heart, and some people even doubt he'll die then, the famous stone in old ireland that cried out when the true king touched it, the fountain of epyrus that could douse lit torches and light unlit ones, women who anointed the fields with their menstrual blood to increase the fertility of the sown seeds, ants the size of dogs, dogs the size of ants, the resurrection on the third day because it couldn't have been on the second. You look very pretty, said the scythe, and it was true, death did look very pretty and she was young, about thirty-six or thirty-seven just as the anthropologists had calculated, You spoke, exclaimed death, There seemed to me to be a good reason, it isn't every day one sees death transformed into the species of which she is the enemy, So it wasn't because you thought I looked pretty, Oh, that too, that too, but I would have spoken even if you'd emerged in the guise of a fat woman in black like the one who appeared to monsieur marcel proust, Well, I'm not fat and I'm not dressed in black, and you have no idea who marcel proust was, For obvious reasons, we scythes, both those who cut down people and those who cut down grass, have never been taught how to read, but we have good memories, mine of blood and theirs of sap, and I've heard proust's name several times and put together the facts, he was a great writer, one of the greatest who ever lived, and his file must be somewhere in the old archives, Yes, but not in mine, I wasn't the death who killed him, So this monsieur marcel proust wasn't from here, then, asked the scythe, No, he was from another country, a place called france, replied death, and there was a touch of sadness in her words, Don't worry, you can console yourself for the fact that it wasn't you who killed proust by how pretty you look today, said the scythe helpfully, As you know, I've always considered you to be a friend, but my sadness has nothing to do with not having been the one to kill proust, What then, Well, I'm not sure I can explain. The scythe gave death a bemused look and thought it best to change the subject, Where did you find the clothes you're wearing, it asked, There are plenty to choose from behind that door, it's like a warehouse, like a vast theatre wardrobe, there are literally hundreds of wardrobes, hundreds of mannequins, thousands of hangers, Take me there, pleaded the scythe, What's the point, you know nothing about fashions or style, Well, one look at you tells me that you don't know much more than I do, the clothes you're wearing don't seem to go together at all, Since you never leave this room, you have no idea what people are wearing these days, That blouse looks very like others I can remember from when I led an active life, Fashions go in cycles, they come and go, they go and come, if I were to tell you what I see out in those streets, No need to tell me, I believe you, Don't you think this blouse goes well with the colour of the trousers and the shoes, Yes, agreed the scythe, And with this cap I'm wearing, Yes, that too, And with this fur coat, Yes, And with this shoulder bag, Yes, you're quite right, And with these earrings, Oh, I give up, Go on, admit it, I'm irresistible, That depends on the kind of man you hope to seduce, But you think I look pretty, That's what I said to begin with, In that case, goodbye, I'll be back on Sunday, or Monday at the latest, don't forget to send off the post each day, that shouldn't be too hard a task for someone who spends all his time leaning against the wall, You've got the letter, asked the scythe, deciding not to rise to such sarcasm, Yes, it's in here, said death, tapping her bag with the tips of slender, well-manicured fingers, which anyone would be pleased to kiss.

Death appeared in daylight in a narrow street, with walls on both sides, almost on the outskirts of the city. There is no door or gate through which she could have emerged, nor is there any clue that would allow us to reconstruct the path that led her from the cold subterranean room to here. The sun doesn't trouble her empty eye sockets, that's why the skulls found in archeological digs have no need to lower their eyelids when the light suddenly strikes their face and the happy anthropologist announces that his bony find shows every sign of being a neanderthal, even though a subsequent examination reveals it to be merely a vulgar homo sapiens. Death, however, this death who has become a woman, takes a pair of dark glasses out of her bag and uses them to protect her now human eyes from the risk of catching a nasty case of conjunctivitis, which is more than likely in someone who has yet to accustom herself to the brightness of a summer morning. Death walks down the street to where the walls end and the first buildings begin. From that point on, she finds herself in familiar territory, there is not one house among these and all the others spread out before her as far as the very limits of city and country that she has not visited at least once, and in two weeks' time she will even have to go into that building under construction over there in order to cause a distracted mason, who fails to notice where he's putting his feet, to fall from the scaffolding. We often say in such cases, that's life, when it would be far more accurate to say, that's death. We wouldn't give that name to the girl in dark glasses who is just getting into a taxi, we would probably think she was the very personification of life and run breathlessly after her, we would tell the driver of another taxi, if there was one, Follow that cab, and there would be no point, because the taxi carrying her off has already turned the corner and there is no other taxi to which we might say, Please, follow that cab. Then we would be quite right in saying, that's life and in giving a resigned shrug. Be that as it may, and let this serve as some consolation, the letter that death is carrying in her bag bears the name of another addressee and another address, our turn to fall from the scaffolding has not yet come. Contrary to what you might reasonably expect, death did not give the taxi driver the cellist's address, but that of the theatre where he performs. It's true that, after her two previous failures, she has decided to play safe, but it was no mere chance that had made her begin by transforming herself into a woman, indeed, as a grammatical soul might be inclined to think, and as we discussed earlier, since both death and woman are female, it was her natural gender. Despite its complete lack of experience of the outside world, particularly as regards feelings, appetites and temptations, the scythe had hit the nail on the head when, at one point in its conversation with death, it had enquired as to what kind of man she hoped to seduce. That was the key word, seduce. Death could have gone straight to the cellist's house, rung the bell and, when he opened the door, thrown him the bait of a charming smile, having first removed her dark glasses, and announced herself, for example, to be a seller of encyclopaedias, a very hackneyed ploy, but one that almost always works, and then he would either invite her in to discuss things quietly over a cup of tea, or he would tell her at once that he wasn't interested and make as if to close the door, at the same time apologising politely for his refusal. I wouldn't want one even if it was a music encyclopaedia, he would say with a shy smile. In either situation, handing over the letter would be an easy matter, almost, we might say, outrageously easy, and that was precisely what death didn't like. The man didn't know her, but she knew him, she had spent a whole night in the same room as him, she had heard him play and, whether you like it or not, such things forge bonds, establish a certain rapport, mark the beginnings of a relationship, and to announce to him bluntly, You're going to die, you have a week in which to sell your cello and find another owner for your dog, would be a brutal act unworthy of the pretty woman she has become. No, she had a different plan.

A poster at the entrance to the theatre informed the worthy public that this week there would be two concerts by the national symphony orchestra, one on thursday, that is, the day after tomorrow, the other on saturday. It's only natural that the curiosity of anyone following this tale with scrupulous and microscopic attention, on the look-out for contradictions, slips, omissions and logical faults, should demand to know how death is going to pay for her tickets to these concerts when only two hours have passed since she emerged from a subterranean room where there are, we believe, no cashpoints or banks with open doors. And now that it's in interrogative vein, that same curiosity will also want to know if taxi drivers no longer charge women who wear dark glasses, have a pleasant smile and a nice body. Before that ill-intentioned suggestion begins to take root, we hasten to say that not only did death pay the amount on the meter, she also gave the driver a tip. As to where that money came from, if this still worries the reader, suffice it to say that it came from the same place as the dark glasses, that is, from the shoulder bag, since, in principle, and as far as we know, there is nothing to stop one thing coming from the same place as another. It could be that the money with which death paid for the taxi and with which she'll pay for the two tickets to the concerts, as well as the hotel where she'll be staying for the next few days, is now out of circulation. It wouldn't be the first time that we go to bed with one kind of money and wake up with another. It must be assumed, therefore, that the money is of good quality and covered by the current legislation, unless, knowing as we do

174

death's talent for mystification, the taxi driver, not noticing that he was being tricked, accepted from the woman in the dark glasses a bank note which is not of this world or, at least, not of this age, bearing the picture of a president of the republic instead of the venerable and familiar face of his majesty the king. The theatre box office has just opened, death goes in, smiles, says good morning and asks for two seats in the best box, one for Thursday and the other for Saturday. She tells the attendant that she wants the same seats for both concerts and, more importantly, that the box should be on the right and as close to the stage as possible. Death stuck her hand into her bag at random, pulled out her purse and handed over what seemed to her the right amount of money. The attendant gave her the change. Here you are, she said, I hope you enjoy the concerts, it's the first time, isn't it, at least I don't remember seeing you before, and I have an excellent memory for people, in fact, I never forget a face, although it's true that glasses do change a person, especially dark glasses like the ones you're wearing. Death took off her glasses, What do you think now, she asked, No, I'm sure I've never seen you before, Perhaps because this is the first time that the person standing here, the person I am now, has ever had to buy tickets for a concert, why, only a few days ago, I had the pleasure of attending an orchestra rehearsal and no one even noticed me, Sorry, I don't understand, Remind me to explain it to you one day, When, Oh, one day, the day that always comes, Now you're frightening me. Death smiled her pretty smile and asked, Tell me frankly, do I look frightening, No, that isn't what I meant at all, Then do as I do, smile and think of nice things, The concert season will last another month yet, Now that is a piece of good news, perhaps we'll see each other next week, then, Well, I'm always here, I'm almost part of the theatre furniture, Don't worry, I'll find you even if you're not, All right, then, I'll expect you, Oh, I'll be there. Death paused and asked, By the way, have you or any of your family received a violet-coloured letter, The letter from death, That's right, No, thank god, but our neighbour's week is up tomorrow and he's in the most terrible state about it, What can we do, that's life, Yes, you're right, sighed the woman, that's life. Fortunately, by then, more people had arrived to buy tickets, otherwise, who knows where this conversation might have led.

Now it's a matter of finding a hotel not too far from the musician's house. Death strolled down into the centre, went into a travel agency, asked if she could study a map of the city, on which she quickly located the theatre, and from there her index finger travelled across the map to the area where the cellist lived. It was a little out of the way, but there were hotels nearby. The assistant recommended one of them, not luxurious, but comfortable. He himself offered to make the reservation over the phone, and when death asked him how much she owed him for his efforts, he replied, smiling, Just put it on my account. What could be more normal, people say things without thinking, they utter words at random and it doesn't even occur to them to consider the consequences, Put it on my account, said the man, doubtless imagining, with incorrigible masculine vanity, some pleasurable encounter in the near future. He risked death replying with a cold eye, Be careful, you don't know who you're talking to, but she merely gave a vague smile, thanked him and set off without leaving a phone number or a visiting card. In the air hung a diffuse perfume, a mixture of rose and chrysanthemum, Yes, that's what it smells like, half rose and half chrysanthemum, murmured the assistant, while he slowly folded up the city map. Out in the street, death was hailing a taxi and giving the driver the address of the hotel. She didn't feel at all pleased with herself. She had frightened the kindly lady in the box office, she'd had fun at her expense, and that's an unforgivable thing to do. People are quite terrified enough of death without her appearing before them with a smile and saying, Hi, it's me, the latest version, the familiar version if you like, of that ominous latin tag memento, homo, quia pulvis es et in pulverem reverteris, and then, as if that weren't enough, she had been about to skewer another extremely nice, helpful person with the stupid question that the so-called upper classes have the barefaced cheek to ask of those beneath them, Do you know who you're talking to. No, death is not pleased with her own behaviour. She is sure that in her skeletal form she would never have behaved like that, Perhaps it's because I've taken on human form, she thought, these things are catching. She glanced out of the window and recognised the street they were driving along, this is the cellist's street and that's the ground-floor apartment where he lives. Death seemed to feel a tightening in her solar plexus, a sudden agitation of the nerves, like the shiver that goes through a hunter when he spies his prey, when he has it within his sights, it could be a kind of obscure fear, as if she were beginning to feel afraid of herself. The taxi stopped, This is the hotel, said the driver. Death paid him with the change that the woman at the theatre had given her, The rest is for you, she said, not even noticing that the rest was more than the amount on the taxi meter. She had an excuse, this is the first time she has used the services of this form of public transport.

As she went over to the reception desk, she remembered that the man at the travel agency hadn't asked her name, he had simply said to the hotel, I'm sending you a customer, yes, a customer, right now, and there she was, this customer who could not possibly say that her name was death, with a small d, please, or that she didn't know what name to give, ah, her bag, the bag over her shoulder, the bag out of which came the dark glasses and the money, the bag out of which must surely come some identifying document, Good afternoon, may I help you, asked the receptionist, A travel agency phoned a quarter of an hour ago to make a reservation for me, Yes, madam, I was the one who took the call, Well, here I am, Would you mind filling out this form, please. Death knows what her name is now, she found it on the identity card that lies open on the desk, and thanks to her dark glasses she will be able to copy down the facts discreetly, name, place of birth, nationality, marital status, profession, without the receptionist realising, Here you are, she said, How long will you be staying at the hotel, Until next Monday, May I make a photocopy of your credit card, Oh, I didn't bring it with me, but I can pay now, in advance, if you like, No, no, that won't be necessary, said the receptionist. She took the identity card to cross-check the information on the form and, with a puzzled expression on her face, glanced up. The photo on the document was that of a much older woman. Death took off her dark glasses and smiled. Confused, the receptionist looked again at the document, the photo and the woman before her were now as alike as two peas in a pod. Do you have any luggage, she asked, drawing one hand across her perspiring brow, No, I came to town to do some shopping, replied death.

She stayed in her room all day, taking both lunch and supper in the hotel. She watched television until late. Then she got into bed and turned out the light. She didn't sleep. Death never sleeps.

WEARING THE NEW DRESS THAT SHE BOUGHT YESTERDAY IN A shop downtown, death goes to the concert. She is sitting alone in the box, and, just as she did during the rehearsal, she is looking at the cellist. Just before the lights went down, when the orchestra was waiting for the conductor to come, he noticed her. He wasn't the only musician to do so. Firstly, because she was alone in the box, which although not rare, wasn't that frequent an occurrence either. Secondly, because she was pretty, possibly not the prettiest woman in the audience, but pretty in a very particular, indefinable way that couldn't be put into words, like a line of poetry whose ultimate meaning, if such a thing exists in a line of poetry, continually escapes the translator. And finally, because her lone figure, there in the box, surrounded by emptiness and absence on every side, as if she inhabited a void, seemed to be the expression of the most absolute solitude. Death, who had smiled so often and so dangerously since she emerged from her icy subterranean room, is not smiling now. The men in the audience observe her with ambiguous curiosity, the women with keen disquiet, but she, like an eagle diving through the air towards a lamb, only has eyes for the cellist. With one difference, though. In the gaze of this other eagle who has always caught her victims there is something like a tenuous veil of pity, eagles, as we know, are obliged to kill, that is their nature, but this eagle here, now, would perhaps prefer, faced by the defenceless lamb, to open her powerful wings and fly back up into the sky, into the cold air of space, into the untouchable flocks of the clouds. The orchestra has fallen silent. The cellist starts to play his solo as if he had been born for that alone. He doesn't know that the woman in the box has in her brand-new handbag a violet-coloured letter addressed to him, he doesn't know, how could he, and yet he plays as if he were bidding farewell to the world, as if he were at last saying everything that he had always kept unsaid, the truncated dreams, the frustrated yearnings, in short, life. The other musicians stare at him in amazement, the conductor with surprise and respect, the audience sighs, a shudder runs through them, and the veil of pity that clouded the sharp gaze of the eagle is now a veil of tears. The solo is over, the orchestra washed over the cello's song like a great, slow sea, gently submerging it, absorbing and amplifying that song as if to lead it into a place where music was transmuted into silence, into the merest shadow of a vibration that touched the skin like the final, inaudible murmur of a kettledrum on which a passing butterfly had momentarily alighted. The silken, malevolent flight of acherontia atropos fluttered quickly through death's memory, but she brushed it away with a wave of her hand which could as easily have been the gesture that made the letters disappear from the desk in her subterranean room as it could a gesture of thanks to the cellist, who was now turning his head in her direction, his eyes seeking a path through the warm darkness of the theatre. Death repeated the gesture and it was as if her slender fingers had perched for a moment on the hand moving the bow. However, even though his heart had done everything to make the cellist miss a note, he did not. Her fingers would not touch him again, death had realised that one must never distract an artist while he is prac-tising his art. When the concert was over and the audience burst into loud cheering, when the lights went up and the conductor brought the orchestra to their feet, and then indicated to the cellist that he alone should get up in order to receive his much-deserved quota of the applause, death, standing, smiling at last, pressed her hands to her breast, in silence, and just looked, that's all, let the others clap, let the others cry bravo, let the others call the conductor back ten times, she just looked. Then, slowly, as if reluctantly, the audience began to leave, at the same time as the orchestra was packing up. When the cellist turned towards the box, she, the woman, was no longer there. Ah, well, that's life, he murmured.

He was wrong, life isn't always like that, the woman from the box will be waiting for him at the stage door. Some of the musicians stare at her intently as they leave, but they realise, without knowing how, that she is surrounded by an invisible hedge, by a high-voltage fence on which they would burn up like tiny moths. Then the cellist appeared. When he saw her, he started, nearly took a step back, as if, seen from close to, the woman was something other than a woman, something from another sphere, another world, from the dark side of the moon. He bowed his head, he tried to join his departing colleagues, to run away, but the cello case, slung over one shoulder, made escape difficult. The woman was there before him, she was saying, Don't run away, I only came to thank you for the excitement and pleasure of hearing you play, That's very kind of you, but I'm just an orchestra player, not a famous concert artiste, the kind for whom fans wait hours just to be able to touch them or ask them for their autograph, If that's the problem, I can ask you for yours, if you like, I haven't got my autograph album with me, but I have here an envelope that would serve perfectly well, No, you misunderstand me, what I meant was that, although I'm flattered by your attention, I don't feel I deserve it, The audience seemed to disagree, Well, I obviously had a good day, Exactly, and that good day just happened to coincide with my appearance here tonight,

Look, I don't want you to think me ungrateful or rude, but probably by tomorrow you'll have got over tonight's excitement, and as suddenly as you appeared, you'll disappear again, You don't know me, I always stick to my resolutions, And what are they, Oh, only one, to meet you, And now that you've met me, we can say goodbye, Are you afraid of me, asked death, No, I just find you rather troubling, And is feeling troubled by my presence such a small thing, Being troubled doesn't necessarily mean being afraid, it might just be a warning to be prudent, Prudence only serves to postpone the inevitable, sooner or later, it surrenders, That won't, I hope, be my case, Oh, I'm sure it will. The cellist moved his cello case from one shoulder to the other, Are you tired, asked the woman, It's not the cello that's heavy, it's the case, especially this one, which is the old-fashioned kind, Look, I need to talk to you, But I don't see how, it's nearly midnight, everyone has left, There are still a few people over there, They're waiting for the conductor, We could talk in a bar, Can you imagine me with a cello on my back walking into a crowded bar, said the cellist, smiling, imagine if all my colleagues went there and took their instruments, We could give another concert, We, asked the musician, intrigued by that plural, Yes, there was a time when I played the violin, there are even pictures of me playing, You seem determined to surprise me with every word you say, It's up to you whether you find out just how surprising I can be, Well, that seems clear enough, That's where you're wrong, I didn't mean what you were thinking, And what was I thinking, may I ask, About bed and me in that bed, Forgive me, No, it was my fault, if I was a man and I'd heard those words, I would certainly have thought the same, one pays the price for ambiguity, Thank you for being so honest. The woman took a few steps and then said, Come on then, Where, asked the cellist, Me to the hotel where I'm staying and you, I imagine, to your apartment, Won't I see you again, So you don't find me troubling any more, Oh, that was nothing, Don't lie, All right, I did find you troubling, but I don't now. On death's face appeared a kind of smile in which there was not a shadow of joy, Now is just when you have most reason to feel troubled, she said, It's a risk I'm willing to take, that's why I'll repeat my question, What was it, Will I see you again, I'll be at the concert on Saturday and I'll be sitting in the same box, It's a different programme, you know, I don't have a solo in it, Yes, I know, You seem to have thought of everything, Indeed, And how will all this end, We're still only at the beginning. A taxi was approaching. The woman hailed it and turned to the cellist, I'll take you home, No, I'll take you to your hotel and then go home from there, Either we do as I say, or I'll take another taxi, Do you always get your own way, Yes, always, You must fail occasionally, god is god and he's done almost nothing but fail, Oh, I could prove to you right now that I never fail, OK, show me, Don't be so stupid, death said abruptly, and there was in her voice an obscure, terrible, underlying threat. The cello was placed in the boot of the taxi. The two passengers spoke not a word during the entire journey. When the taxi stopped, the cellist said before he got out, I simply can't understand what's going on between you and me, and I think it would be best if we didn't see each other again, No one can stop it now, Not even you, the woman who always gets her own way, asked the cellist, trying to be ironic, Not even me, replied the woman, So that means you'll fail then, No, it means I won't fail. The driver had got out to open the boot and was waiting for the cellist to remove his cello case. The man and the woman didn't say goodbye, they didn't say see you on Saturday, they didn't touch, it was a heartfelt parting of the ways, dramatic and brutal, as if they had sworn on blood and water never to meet again. Carrying his cello, the musician stalked off and went into the apartment block. He didn't turn round, not even when he paused for an instant on the very threshold. The woman was watching him, clutching her bag. The taxi drove on.

The cellist went into his apartment, muttering angrily, She's mad, barking mad, the one time in my life when someone comes and waits for me at the stage door to say how well I played and she turns out to be a nutter, and I, like a fool, ask if I'll see her again, I'm just creating problems for myself, I mean, really, there are some character defects that perhaps deserve a bit of respect, or are, at least, worthy of one's attention, but stupidity is just ridiculous, infatuation is ridiculous, I was ridiculous. He distractedly patted the dog who had run to greet him at the front door and then went into the piano room. He opened the cello case and carefully removed the instrument, which he would have to retune before going to bed, because journeys in taxis, however short, weren't good for its health. He went into the kitchen to give the dog some food, and prepared himself a sandwich, which he washed down with a glass of wine. He was feeling less annoyed now, but the feeling that was gradually replacing that annoyance was no less disquieting. He remembered things the woman had said, her allusion to ambiguities that always have a price, and he discovered that every word she had said, although each one made perfect sense in context, seemed to carry within it another meaning, something he couldn't quite grasp, something tantalising, like the water that slips away from us when we try to drink it, like the branch that suddenly moves out of reach when we go to pluck the fruit. I wouldn't say she was mad, he thought, but she's certainly odd, there's no doubt about that. He finished his sandwich and returned to the music room or piano room, the two names we have given it up until now, when it would be far more logical to call it the cello room, since that is the instrument by which the musician earns his living, but we have to admit that it wouldn't sound right, it would be slightly degrading, slightly undignified, you just have to follow the descending scale to grasp our reasoning, music room, piano room, cello room, so far, so acceptable, but imagine if we were to start referring to the clarinet room, the fife room, the bass drum room, the triangle room. Words have their own hierarchy, their own protocol, their own aristocratic titles, their own plebeian stigmas. The dog joined his master and lay down beside him having first turned round and round three times, which was the only memory he still retained of the days when he was a wolf. The musician was tuning his cello to the A of the tuning fork, lovingly restoring the instrument's harmonies after the brutal treatment inflicted on it by the taxi rattling over the cobblestones. For a few moments, he had managed to forget the woman at the theatre, not her exactly, but the troubling conversation they'd had at the stage door, although their final tense exchange of words in the taxi continued to be heard in the background, like a muffled roll on the drums. He couldn't forget the woman, he didn't want to. He could see her standing up, her two hands pressed to her breast, he could feel the touch of her intense gaze, hard as a diamond, and how it shone when she smiled. He would see her again on Saturday, he thought, yes, he would see her then, but she would not stand up again, nor press her hands to her breast, nor look at him from afar, that magical moment had been swallowed up, undone by the moment that followed, when he turned to see her for the last time, or so he thought, and she was no longer there.

When the tuning fork had returned to silence and the cello was once more in tune, the phone rang. The musician started, he looked at the watch, it was half past one. Who can be ringing at this hour, he wondered. He picked up the receiver and waited for a few seconds. It was absurd, of course, he was the one who should speak and give his name or number, then someone would probably say at the other end, Oh, sorry, I must have misdialled, but the voice that spoke asked instead, Is it the dog answering the phone, if it is, could he, please, at least bark. The cellist replied, Yes, it is the dog, but I stopped barking a long time ago, I've lost the habit of biting too, apart from biting myself when life plays tricks on me, Don't be angry, I'm phoning to apologise, our conversation took a dangerous turn, and the result, as you saw, was disastrous, Well, someone took it off along that dangerous turn, and it wasn't me, It was my fault entirely, usually I'm very balanced and calm, You didn't seem to me to be either of those things, Perhaps I suffer from a split personality, That makes us equal then, I myself am both dog and man, Irony doesn't suit you, but your musical ear will doubtless already have told you that, Dissonance also has a role to play in music, ma'am, Don't call me ma'am, How else should I address you, since I don't know your name or what you do or what you are, You'll find out eventually, remember, haste makes a bad counsellor, besides, we've only just met, You're one step ahead of me, though, since you have my phone number, That's what directory enquiries is for, the receptionist found it for me, It's a shame this is such an old phone, Why, Because if it was one of those modern ones, I'd know where you were phoning from, I'm phoning from my hotel room, That much I knew, And as for the antiquity of your phone, I assumed that would be the case, so it doesn't surprise me in the least, Why, Because everything about you seems old-fashioned, it's as if you weren't fifty, but five hundred years old, How do you know I'm fifty, Because I'm very good at guessing people's ages, I never fail, It seems to me that you boast too much about never failing, Yes, you're right, today, for example, I failed twice, something which, I can assure you, has never happened before, Sorry,

I don't understand, You see I have a letter to give you and I failed to do so, although I could easily have given it to you either outside the theatre or in the taxi, What letter is that, Let's just say that I wrote it after attending the rehearsal for your concert, You were there, Yes, I was, But I didn't see you, Of course not, you couldn't, Anyway, it's not my concert, As modest as ever, And saying let's just say isn't the same as saying what actually happened, Sometimes it is, But not in this case, Congratulations, you're not only modest, you're very perceptive too, What letter do you mean, You'll find out in time, So why didn't you give it to me if you had the opportunity, Two opportunities, Exactly, so why didn't you give it to me, That's what I hope to find out, maybe I'll give it to you on Saturday, after the concert, because by Monday I'll be gone, You don't live here, Not what you would call live, no, You've lost me, talking to you is like finding oneself in a labyrinth with no doors, Now that's an excellent definition of life, But you're not life, No, I'm much more complicated than that, Someone wrote that we are all of us life, for the moment, Yes, for the moment, but only for the moment, Let's just hope all this confusion is cleared up the day after tomorrow, the letter, the reason why you didn't give it to me, everything, I'm tired of mysteries, What you call mysteries are often intended as protection, Well, protection or not, I want to see that letter, If I don't fail a third time, you will, And why would you fail a third time, If I do, it could only be for the same reason I failed before, Please, don't play cat and mouse with me, In that particular game, the cat always ends up catching the mouse, Unless the mouse manages to put a bell around the cat's neck, A good answer, but that's just a silly dream, a cartoon fantasy, even if the cat were asleep, the noise would wake it, and then goodbye mouse, Am I the mouse you're saying goodbye to, If we were playing that game, then one of us would have to be the mouse, and you don't seem to me to have either the looks or the cunning to be the cat, So I'm condemned to being a mouse for the rest of my life, For as long as that lasts, yes, a mouse cellist, Another cartoon character, Don't you think all human beings are just cartoon characters, You too, I suppose, You've seen what I look like, A very pretty woman, Thank you, Anyone listening in to this conversation would think we were flirting, If the hotel's telephonist amuses herself by eavesdropping on guests' conversations, she'll already have reached the same conclusion, Even if we are flirting, it won't have any serious consequences, the woman in the box, whose name I still don't know, will be leaving on Monday, Never again to return, Are you sure, It's unlikely that the reasons that brought me here will ever be repeated, Unlikely doesn't meant impossible, No, but I'll do all I can not to have to repeat the journey, It was worth it, though, despite everything, Despite what exactly, Forgive me, I was being indelicate, what I meant to say was, Please, don't bother being nice to me, I'm not used to it, besides, I can guess what you were going to say, but if you feel you owe me a more complete explanation, perhaps we can continue this conversation on Saturday, So I won't see you before that, No. The line was cut. The cellist looked at the receiver still in his hand, which was damp with anxiety, I must be dreaming, he muttered, this isn't the kind of thing that happens to me. He put the receiver down and addressing the piano, the cello and the shelves, he asked, this time out loud, What does this woman want of me, who is she, why has she appeared in my life. Woken by the noise, the dog looked up at him. There was an answer in his eyes, but the cellist didn't notice, he paced the room from one side to the other, feeling even more nervous than before, and the answer was this, Now that you mention it, I do have a vague recollection of having slept in a woman's lap and it might have been hers, What lap, what woman, the cellist would have asked, You were asleep, Where, In your bed, And where was she, Over there, That's a good one, mister dog, how long has it been since a woman came into this apartment, into that bedroom, go on, tell me, As you should know, a dog's perception of time is not the same as that of a human being, but it seems to me that it really has been an age since you last received a lady in your bed, and I don't mean that ironically, So you dreamed it, Probably, we dogs are incorrigible dreamers, we even dream with our eyes open, we just have to see something in the shadows and we immediately imagine that it's a woman's lap and jump onto it, Mere doggy imaginings, the cellist would say, Even if that's true, the dog would reply, we're not complaining. Meanwhile, in her hotel room, death is standing naked before the mirror. She doesn't know who she is.

The following day, the woman didn't phone. The cellist waited in just in case. The evening passed, and not a word. The cellist slept even worse than he had the night before. On Saturday morning, before setting off to his rehearsal, a mad idea occurred to him, to go and ask around all the hotels in the area to see if they had a female guest with her figure, her smile, her way of moving her hands, but he immediately gave up this crazy project, because it was obvious that he would be dismissed with an air of ill-disguised suspicion and an abrupt We are not authorised to give that information. The rehearsal went reasonably well, he merely played what was there on the page, doing his best not to play too many wrong notes. When it was over, he rushed back home. He was thinking that if she had phoned in his absence, she wouldn't even have found a miserable answering machine to record her message. I'm not a man born five centuries ago, I'm a troglodyte from the stone age, everyone uses answerphones except me, he muttered. If he needed proof that she hadn't phoned, the next few hours provided it. In principle, someone who had phoned and got no reply would call again, but the wretched machine remained silent all afternoon, indifferent to the cellist's ever more desperate looks. All right, so it looks like she won't get in touch, perhaps for one reason or another she hasn't had the chance, but she'll be there at the concert, they'll come back together in the same taxi, as happened after the last concert, and when they arrive here, he'll invite her in, and then they can talk calmly, she'll finally give him the longed-for letter and then they'll both laugh at the exaggerated words of praise which she, swept away by artistic enthusiasm, had written after the rehearsal where he hadn't seen her, and he'll say that he's certainly no rostropovich, and she'll say who knows what the future may hold, and when they run out of things to say or when the words start to go one way and their thoughts another, then we'll see if something happens that will be worth remembering in our old age. It was in this state of mind that the cellist left home, it was this state of mind that carried him to the theatre, with this state of mind that he went on stage and sat down in his usual place. The box was empty. She's late, he said to himself, she must be just about to arrive, there are still people coming into the theatre. This was true, the late arrivals were taking their seats, apologising for disturbing those already seated, but the woman did not appear. Perhaps in the interval. She still didn't come. The box remained empty until the end of the perform-ance. Nevertheless, there was a reasonable hope that, having been unable to attend the concert, for reasons she would explain, she'll be waiting for him outside, at the stage door. She wasn't there. And since the fate of hopes is always to breed more hopes, which is why, despite so many disappointments, they have not yet died out in the world, she might be waiting for him outside his building with a smile on her lips and the letter in her hand, Here you are, as promised. She wasn't there either. The cellist went into his apartment like an old-fashioned, first-generation automaton, the sort that had to ask one leg to move in order to move the other one. He pushed away the dog who had come to greet him, put his cello down in the first convenient place and went and lay on his bed. Now will you learn your lesson, you idiot, you've behaved like a complete imbecile, you gave the meanings you wanted to words which, in the end, meant something else entirely, meanings that you don't know and never will know, you believed in smiles that were nothing but deliberate muscular contractions, you forgot that you're really five hundred years old, even though the years very kindly reminded you of this, and now here you are, washed up, lying on the bed where you were hoping to welcome her, while she's laughing at the foolish figure you cut and at your ineradicable stupidity. His master's rebuff forgotten, the dog came over to the bed to console him. He put his front paws on the mattress and pulled himself up to the height of his master's left hand, which lay there like something futile and vain, and gently rested his head on it. He could have licked it and licked it again, as is the way with ordinary dogs, but nature had, for once, revealed her benevolent side and reserved for him a very special sensitivity, one that allowed him even to invent different gestures to express emotions that are always the same and always unique. The cellist turned towards the dog, and adjusted his position so that his head was only a few inches from the dog's head, and there they stayed, looking at each other, saying, with no need for words, When I think about it, I have no idea who you are, but that's not important, what matters is that we care about each other. The cellist's bitterness gradually ebbed away, the fact is the world is full of such episodes, he waited and she never arrived, she waited and he never came, and just between ourselves, unbelieving sceptics that we are, rather that than a broken leg. This is easy enough to say, but it's best not to, because words often have very different effects from those intended, so much so that these men and women quite often curse and swear, I hate her, I hate him, then burst into tears when they've done so. The cellist sat up in bed, put his arms around the dog, which, in a final gesture of solidarity, had placed his paws on his master's knees, and said, like someone telling himself off, A little dignity, please, no whingeing. Then, to the dog he said, You must be hungry. Wagging his tail, the dog replied, Yes, I am hungry, I haven't eaten for hours, and the two went into the kitchen. The cellist didn't eat, he didn't feel like it. Besides, the lump in his throat wouldn't allow him to swallow. Half an hour later, he was back in bed, having taken a pill to help him sleep, not that it did much good. He kept waking and sleeping, waking and sleeping, always with the same obsessive idea that he should be running after sleep to catch it up and thus prevent insomnia from occupying the other side of the bed. He didn't dream about the woman, but there was a moment when he woke and saw her standing in the middle of the music room, with her hands pressed to her breast.

The next day was Sunday, and Sunday is the day he takes the dog for a walk. Love repays love, the animal seemed to be saying, with his lead in his mouth and eager to be off. They entered the park, and the cellist was just heading towards the bench where he usually sat, when he saw that a woman was already sitting there. Park benches are free, public and, usually, gratis, we can't say to someone who arrives before us, This bench is mine, kindly find another one. A well-brought-up man like the cellist would never do that, and certainly not if he thought he recognised that person as the woman from the theatre, the woman who had stood him up, the woman he had seen in the middle of the music room with her two hands pressed to her breast. As we know, at fifty, we can't always trust our eyes, we start to blink, to screw them up as if we were trying to imitate the heroes of the wild west or the navigators of long ago, on top of a horse or at the prow of a caravel, one hand shading their eyes as they scan distant horizons. The woman is dressed differently, in trousers and a leather jacket, she must be someone else, says the cellist to his heart, but his heart, which has better eyesight, tells him, open your eyes, it's her, now you behave yourself. The woman looked up, and the cellist knew for certain then that it was her. Good morning, he said, when he stopped by the bench, the last thing I would have expected today was to find you here, Good morning, I came to say goodbye and to apologise for not coming to the concert yesterday. The cellist sat down, removed the dog's lead, said, Off you go, and without looking at the woman, replied, There's nothing to apologise for, that sort of thing is always happening, people buy a ticket and then, for one reason or another, they can't go, it's perfectly normal, And about our saying goodbye, do you have any views on that, asked the woman, It's extremely kind of you to think that you should come and say goodbye to a stranger, although I really can't imagine how you could possibly know that I come to this park every Sunday, There are very few things I don't know about you, Oh, please, let's not go back to the absurd conversations we had on Thursday at the stage door and afterwards on the phone, you don't know anything about me, we'd never even met before then, Remember, I was at the rehearsal, And I really don't know how you managed that, because the maestro is very strict about strangers being present, and please don't go telling me now that you know him too, Not as well as I know you, but you are an exception, It would be better if I wasn't, Why, Do you want me to tell you, do you really want me to tell you, asked the cellist with a vehemence that bordered on despair, Yes, I do, Because I've fallen in love with a woman I know nothing about, who is amusing herself at my expense, who will go off tomorrow who knows where, and who I'll never see again, It's actually today that I'll be leaving, not tomorrow, But you said, And it isn't true that I've been amusing myself at your expense, Well, if you haven't, you certainly did an excellent imitation, As for you falling in love with me, you can hardly expect me to respond, there are certain words my mouth is forbidden to speak, Another mystery, And it won't be the last, Once we've said goodbye, all the mysteries will be resolved, Others might take their place, Please, go away, don't torment me any more, The letter, Look, I don't want to know anything about the letter, The fact is I couldn't give it to you even if I wanted to, I left it at the hotel, said the woman, smiling, Then tear it up, Yes, I'll have to think what to do with it, There's no need to think, tear it up and be done with it. The woman got to her feet. Are you leaving already, asked the cellist. He hadn't moved, he was sitting with his head bowed, he still had something to say. I've never even touched you, he murmured, No, I was the the one who stopped you touching me, How did you manage that, It wasn't that difficult, Not even now, Not even now, We could at least shake hands, My hands are cold. The cellist looked up. The woman was no longer there.

Man and dog left the park early, the sandwiches were bought to eat at home, there were no naps in the sun. The afternoon and evening were long and sad, the musician picked up a book, read half a page, then threw it down. He sat at the piano to play a little, but his hands would not obey him, they were clumsy, cold, as if dead. And when he returned to his beloved cello, it was the instrument itself that rejected him. He dozed in a chair, hoping to fall into an endless sleep, never to wake again. Lying on the floor, waiting for a sign that did not come, the dog was looking at him. Perhaps the reason for his master's despondency was the woman they had met in the park, he thought, so it wasn't true what the proverb said, that what the eyes don't see, the heart doesn't grieve over. Proverbs are so deceiving, concluded the dog. It was eleven o'clock when the doorbell rang. Some neighbour with a problem, thought the cellist, and got up to open the door. Good evening, said the woman, standing on the threshold. Good evening, replied the musician, trying hard to control the spasm making his throat tighten, Aren't you going to ask me in, Of course, please, come in. He stepped aside to allow her to pass, then closed the door, moving very slowly and carefully, so that his heart would not burst. Legs shaking, he invited her to take a seat. I thought you would have left already, he said, As you see, I decided to stay, said the woman, But you'll leave tomorrow, That's what I've agreed, You've come, I presume, to bring the letter, which you decided not to tear up, Yes, I have it here in my bag, Are you going to give it to me, then, We have time, I remember telling you that haste was a bad counsellor, As you wish, I'm at your disposal, Are you serious, That's my worst defect, I say everything seriously, even when I make people laugh, no, especially when I make people laugh, In that case, may I ask you a favour, What's that, Make it up to me for having missed yesterday's concert, How can I do that, The piano's over there, Oh, forget it, I'm a very mediocre pianist, The cello then, Now that's another matter, I can play you a couple of pieces if you really want me to, May I choose the music, asked the woman, Yes, but only if it's something I can play, that's within my range. The woman chose the sheet music for bach's suite number six and said, This, It's very long, it takes more than half an hour, and it's getting late, As I said, we have time, There's a passage in the prelude that I always have difficulties with, It doesn't matter, you could just miss it out when you get there, said the woman, although that won't be necessary, you'll see, you'll play even better than rostropovich. The cellist smiled, You bet. He placed the sheet music on the stand, took a deep breath, placed his left hand on the neck of the cello, his right hand holding the bow poised over the strings, and then he began. He knew perfectly well that he was no rostropovich, that he was only an orchestra soloist when the programme happened to require this of him, but here, sitting opposite this woman, with his dog lying at his feet, at that late hour of the night, surrounded by books, sheet music, scores, he was johann sebastian bach himself composing in cöthen what would later be called opus one thousand and twelve, almost as many as the works of creation. He got through the difficult passage without even noticing this great feat, his happy hands made the cello murmur, speak, sing, roar, this is what rostropovich had lacked, this room, this hour, this woman. When he finished playing, her hands were no longer cold and his hands were on fire, which is why their hands were not in the least surprised when hand reached out to hand. It was long after one o'clock in the morning when the cellist asked, Would you like me to call you a taxi to take you back to the hotel, and the woman replied, No, I'll stay here with you, and she offered him her mouth. They went into the bedroom, got undressed, and what was written would happen finally happened, and again, and yet again. He fell asleep, she did not. Then she, death, got up, opened the bag she had left in the music room and took out the violet-coloured letter. She looked around for a place where she could leave it, on the piano, between the strings of the cello, or else in the bedroom itself, under the pillow on which the man's head was resting. She did none of these things. She went into the kitchen, lit a match, a humble match, she who could make the paper vanish with a single glance and reduce it to an impalpable dust, she who could set fire to it with the mere touch of her fingers, and yet it was a simple match, an ordinary match, an everyday match, that set light to death's letter, the letter that only death could destroy. No ashes remained. Death went back to bed, put her arms around the man and, without understanding what was happening to her, she who never slept felt sleep gently closing her eyelids. The following day, no one died.